Katie
and the
cupcake
cure

This book is a work of fiction. Any references to historical events, real people, or real places are used fictitiously. Other names, characters, places, and events are products of the author's imagination, and any resemblance to actual events or places or persons, living or dead, is entirely coincidental.

SIMON SPOTLIGHT
An imprint of Simon & Schuster Children's Publishing Division
1230 Avenue of the Americas, New York, New York 10020
Copyright © 2011 by Simon & Schuster, Inc.
First Simon Spotlight hardcover edition 2013
All rights reserved, including the right of reproduction
in whole or in part in any form.
SIMON SPOTLIGHT and colophon are registered
trademarks of Simon & Schuster, Inc.
Text by Tracey West
Chapter header illustrations and design by Laura Roode
For information about special discounts for bulk purchases, please contact
Simon & Schuster Special Sales
at 1-866-506-1949 or business@simonandschuster.com.
Manufactured in the United States of America 0413 FFG
First Edition
2 4 6 8 10 9 7 5 3 1
ISBN 978-1-4424-7490-1 (hc)
ISBN 978-1-4424-2275-9 (pbk)
ISBN 978-1-4424-2276-6 (eBook)
Library of Congress Catalog Card Number 2010940448

CUPCAKE DIARIES

Katie

and the

cupcake

cure

by coco simon

Simon Spotlight

New York   London   Toronto   Sydney   New Delhi

CHAPTER 1

Who's Afraid of Middle School? Not Me!

Every time I have ever watched a movie about middle school, the main character is always freaking out before the first day of school. You know what I mean, right? If the movie's about a guy, he's always worried about getting stuffed into a garbage can by jocks. If it's about a girl, she's trying on a zillion outfits and screaming when she sees a pimple on her face. And no matter what movie it is, the main character is always obsessed with being popular.

My name is Katie Brown, and whenever I watched those movies, I just didn't get it. I mean, how could middle school be *that* different from elementary school? Yeah, I knew there would be new kids from other schools, but I figured everyone from our school would stick together. We've all pretty much known one another since kinder-garten. Sure, not everybody hangs out together, but it's not like we put some kids on a pedestal and worship them or anything. We're all the same. Back in third grade, we all got sick together on mystery meat loaf day. That kind of experience has to bind you for life, doesn't it?

That's what I thought, anyway. I didn't spend one single second of the summer worrying about middle school. I got a really bad sunburn at the town pool, made a thousand friendship bracelets at day camp, and learned from my mom how to make a cake that looks like an American flag. I didn't stress out about middle school at all.

Guess what? I was wrong! But you probably knew that already. Yeah, the cruel hammer of real-ity hit pretty hard on the very first day of school. And the worst thing was, I wasn't even expecting it.

The morning started out normal. I put on the tie-dyed T-shirt I made at day camp, my favor-ite pair of jeans, and a new pair of white sneak-ers. Then I slipped about ten friendship bracelets on each arm, which I thought looked pretty cool. I brushed my hair, which takes about thirty sec-onds. My hair is brown and wavy—Mom calls it au naturel. I only worry about my hair when it starts to hang in my eyes, and then I cut it.

When I went downstairs for breakfast, Mom was waiting for me in the kitchen.

"Happy first day of middle school, Katie!" she shouted.

Did I mention that my mom is supercorny? I think it's because she's a dentist. I read a survey once that said that people are afraid of dentists more than anything else, even zombies and funeral directors. (Which is totally not fair, because without dentists everybody would have rotten teeth, and without teeth you can't eat corn on the cob, which is delicious.) But anyway, I think she tries to smile all the time and make jokes so that people will like her more. Not that she's fake—she's honestly pretty nice, for a mom.

"I made you a special breakfast," Mom told me. "A banana pancake shaped like a school bus!"

The pancake sat on a big white plate. Mom had used banana slices for wheels and square pieces of cantaloupe for the windows. This might seem like a strange breakfast to you, but my mom does stuff like this all the time. She wanted to go to cooking school when she got out of high school, but her parents wanted her to be a dentist, like them. Which is unfair, except that if she didn't go to dental school, she wouldn't have met my dad, and I would never have been born, so I guess I can't complain.

But anyway, in her free time she does the whole Martha Stewart thing. Not that she looks like Martha Stewart. She has brown hair like me, but hers is curly, and her favorite wardrobe items are her blue dentist coat and her apron that says #1 CHEF on the front. This morning she was wearing both.

"Thanks, Mom," I said. I didn't say anything about being too old for a pancake shaped like a school bus. It would have hurt her feelings. Besides, it was delicious.

She sat down in the seat next to me and sipped her coffee. "Do you have the map I printed out for you with the new bus stop location?" she asked me. She was doing that biting-her-bottom-lip thing she does when she's worried about me, which is most of the time.

"I got it, but I don't need it," I replied. "It's only four blocks away."

Mom frowned. "Okay. But I e-mailed the map to Barbara just in case."

Barbara is my mom's best friend—and she's also the mom of my own best friend, Callie. We've known each other since we were babies. Callie is two months older than I am, and she never lets me forget it.

"I hope Callie has the map," my mom went on. "I wouldn't want you two to get lost on your first day of middle school."

"We won't," I promised. "I'm meeting Callie at the corner of Ridge Street, and we're walking to the bus stop together."

"Oh, good," Mom said. "I'm glad you finally talked to your old bus buddy."

"Uh, yeah," I said, and quickly gulped down some orange juice. I hadn't actually talked to her. But we'd been bus buddies ever since kindergarten (my corny mom came up with "bus buddies," in case you didn't figure that out already), so there was no real reason to believe this year would be any different. I knew I'd see her at the bus stop.

Every August, Callie goes to sleepaway camp, which totally stinks. She doesn't get back until a few days before school starts. Normally I see her the first day she comes back and we go to King Cone for ice cream.

But this year Callie texted that she was busy shopping with her mom. Callie has always cared a lot more about clothes than I do. She wanted to find the perfect outfit to wear on her first day of middle school. And since we only had a few days before school started I didn't think it was *that* weird that I didn't see her. It was a *little* weird that she hadn't called me back. But we had texted and agreed to meet on the corner of Ridge Street, so I was sure everything was fine.

I ate my last bite of pancake and stood up. "Gotta brush my teeth," I said. When you're the daughter of a dentist, you get into that habit pretty early.

Soon I was slipping on my backpack and heading for the door. Of course, Mom grabbed me and gave me a big hug.

"I packed you a special lunch, Cupcake," she said.

Mom has called me Cupcake ever since I can remember. I kind of like it—except when she says it in front of other people.

"A special lunch? Really?" I teased her. Every lunch she makes me is a special lunch. "What a surprise."

"I love you!" Mom called. I turned and waved. For a second I thought she was going to follow me to the bus so I yelled, "I love you too!" and ran down the driveway.

Outside, it still felt like summer. *I should have worn shorts,* I thought. There's nothing worse than sitting in a hot classroom sweating a lot and having your jeans stick to your legs. Gross. But it was too late to change now.

Ridge Street was only two blocks away. There were lots of kids heading for the bus stop, but I didn't see Callie. I stood on the corner, tapping my foot.

"Come on, Callie," I muttered. If we missed the bus, Mom would insist on walking me to the bus stop every morning. I didn't know if I could take that much cheerfulness before seven thirty a.m.

Then a group of girls turned the corner: Sydney Whitman, Maggie Rodriguez, and Brenda Kovacs—and Callie was with them! I was a little confused. Callie usually didn't walk with them. It was always just Callie and me.

"Hey, Cal!" I called out.

Callie looked up at me and waved, but continued talking to Maggie.

That was strange. I noticed, though, she wasn't wearing her glasses. She's as blind as a bat without her glasses. *Maybe she doesn't recognize me,* I reasoned. *My hair did get longer this summer.*

So I ran up to them. That's when I noticed they were all dressed kind of alike—even Callie. They were wearing skinny jeans and each girl had on a different color T-shirt and a thick belt.

"Hey, guys," I said. "The bus stop's this way." I nodded toward Ridge Street.

Callie looked at me and smiled. "Hi, Katie! We were just talking about walking to school," she said.

"Isn't it kind of far to walk?" I asked.

Maggie spoke up. "Only little kids take the bus."

"Oh," I said. (I know, I sound like a genius. But I was thinking about how my mom probably wouldn't like the idea of us walking to school.)

Then Sydney looked me up and down. "Nice shirt, Katie," she said. But she said it in a way that I knew meant she definitely didn't think it was nice. "Did you make that at camp?"

Maggie and Brenda giggled.

"As a matter of fact, I did," I said.

I looked at Callie. I didn't say anything. She didn't say anything. What was going on?

"Come on," Sydney said, linking arms with Callie. "I don't want to be late."

She didn't say, "Come on, everybody but Katie," but she might as well have. I knew I wasn't invited. Callie turned around and waved. "See you later!" she called.

I stood there, frozen, as my best friend walked away from me like I was some kind of stranger.

CHAPTER 2

The Horrible Truth Hits Me

*Y*ou might think I was mad at Callie. But I wasn't. Well, not really. For the most part I was really confused.

Why didn't Callie ask me to walk with them? Something had to be going on. Like, maybe her mom had told her to walk with those girls for some reason. Or maybe Callie didn't ask me to walk with them because she figured I would be the one to ask. Maybe that was it.

The sound of a bus engine interrupted my thoughts. Two blocks away, I could see a yellow school bus turning the corner. I was going to miss it!

I tore off down the sidewalk. It's a good thing I'm a fast runner because I got to the bus stop just as the last kid was getting on board. I climbed up the steps, and the bus driver gave me a nod. She was a friendly-looking woman with a round face and curly black hair.

It hit me for the first time that I would have a new bus driver now that I was going to middle school. The elementary school bus driver, Mr. Hopkins, was really nice. And I might never see him again!

But I couldn't think about that now. I had to find a place to sit. Callie and I always sat in the third seat down on the right. Two boys I didn't know were sitting in that seat. I stood there, staring at the seats, not knowing what to do.

"Please find a seat," the bus driver told me.

I walked down the aisle. Maybe there was something in the back. As I passed the sixth row, a girl nodded to the empty seat next to her. I quickly slid into it, and the bus lurched forward.

"Thanks," I said.

"No problem," replied the girl. "I'm Mia."

I don't really know a lot about fashion, but I could tell that Mia was wearing stuff that you see in magazines. She could even have been a model herself—she had long black hair that wasn't dull like mine, but shiny and bouncy. She was wearing those leggings that look like jeans, with black boots, and a short black jacket over a long gray T-shirt. I figured that Mia must be a popular girl from one of the other elementary schools.

"Are you from Richardson?" I asked her. "I used to go to Hamilton."

Mia shook her head. "I just moved here a few weeks ago. From Manhattan."

"Mia from Manhattan. That's easy to remember," I said. I started talking a mile a minute, like I do when I'm nervous or excited. "I never met anyone who lived in Manhattan before. I've only been there once. We saw *The Lion King* on Broadway. I just remember it was really crowded and really noisy. Was it noisy where you lived?"

"My neighborhood was pretty quiet," Mia replied.

I suddenly realized that my question might have been insulting.

"Not that noisy is bad," I said quickly. "I just meant—you know, the cars and buses and people and stuff . . ." I decided I wasn't making things any better.

But Mia didn't seem to mind. "You're right. It can get pretty crazy. But I like it there," she said. "I still live there, kind of. My dad does, anyway."

Were her parents divorced like mine? I wondered.

I wanted to ask her, but it seemed like a really personal question. I chose a safer subject. "So, how do you like Maple Grove?"

"It's pretty here," she answered. "It's just kind of . . . quiet."

She smiled, and I smiled back. "Yeah, things can be pretty boring around here," I said.

"By the way, I like your shirt," Mia told me. "Did you make it yourself?"

I got a sick feeling for a second—was she making fun of me, like Sydney had? But the look on her face told me she was serious.

"Thanks," I said, relieved. "I'm glad you said that because somebody earlier didn't like it at all, and what was extra weird is that my best friend was hanging around with that person."

"That sounds complicated," Mia said.

That's when the bus pulled into the big round driveway in front of Park Street Middle School. I'd seen the school a million times before, of course, since it was right off the main road. And I'd been inside once, last June, when the older kids had given us a tour. I just remember thinking how much bigger it was than my elementary school. The guide leading us kept saying it was shaped like a *U* so it was easy to get around. But it didn't seem easy to me.

We climbed out of the bus, which had stopped in front of the wide white steps that led up to the front door. The concrete building was the color of beach sand, and for a second I wished it was still summer and I was back on the beach.

Mia took a piece of yellow paper out of her jacket pocket. "My homeroom is in room 212," she said. "What's yours?"

I shrugged off my backpack. My schedule was somewhere inside. I zipped it open and started searching through my folders.

"I've got to find mine," I said. "Go on ahead."

"Are you sure?" Mia looked hesitant. If I hadn't been freaking out about my schedule, I might have noticed that she didn't want to go in alone. But I wasn't thinking too clearly.

"Yeah," I said. "I'll see you later!"

After what seemed forever I finally found my schedule tucked inside one of the pockets of my five-subject notebook. I looked on the line that read HOMEROOM . . . 216.

So I wouldn't be with Mia. But would I be with Callie? She and I had meant to go over our schedules to see what classes we'd have together. Now I didn't know if we had the same gym or lunch or anything.

Maybe we're in the same homeroom, I thought hopefully. I studied the little map on the bottom of the schedule and went inside. From the front door, it was pretty easy to find room 216. It looked like a social studies classroom, I guessed. There were maps of the world on the wall and a big globe in the corner. I scanned the room for Callie, but I didn't see her, although Maggie and Brenda were there, sitting next to each other. Almost all of the seats were taken; the only empty ones were in the front row, where nobody ever wants to sit. But I had no choice.

I purposely took the seat in front of Maggie— partly because I knew her from my old school, and partly because I wanted to get some info about Callie.

I set my backpack on the floor and turned around. Maggie and Brenda were drawing with gel pens on their notebooks. They were both tracing the letters "PGC" in big bubble print. When they saw me looking, they quickly flipped over their notebooks.

"Hey," I said. "Do you know if Callie is in this homeroom?"

"Why don't you ask her yourself?" Maggie asked, and Brenda burst out into giggles.

"Um, okay," I said, but I could feel my face getting red. Callie and I had never hung out with Sydney, Maggie, and Brenda at our old school, but they had always been basically nice. At least, they'd never been mean to me.

But I guess things had changed.

The bell rang, and for the first time, I felt a pang of middle school fear. Just like those kids in the movies.

It was a horrible thought, but I knew it was true.... Middle school wasn't going to be as easy as I'd hoped!

CHAPTER 3

Humiliated in Homeroom!

$\mathscr{L}$uckily, the homeroom teacher walked in before Maggie or Brenda could say anything else. Mr. Insley had dark brown hair and a beard and mustache.

"Welcome to homeroom," he said, smiling. "This room will be your first stop every morning before you head out to your classes. I can guarantee that this will be your easiest class of the day. On most days, we only have three things to do: take attendance, say the Pledge of Allegiance, and listen to announcements."

"Yeah, no homework!" a boy in the back of the room called out.

"You'll get plenty of that in your other classes," Mr. Insley said, and a bunch of kids groaned. I had to admit that it made me nervous. I had heard that there was tons more homework in middle school, but I hoped it wasn't true.

"Today is your lucky day, because you get to have homeroom with me for an extra ten minutes," Mr. Insley went on. "I'll be giving you some tips about how to get around this place."

There was a loud beeping sound over the inter-com.

"Good morning, students! This is Principal LaCosta. Welcome to Park Street Middle School. Please stand for the Pledge of Allegiance."

We launched into the pledge, and after the principal made a few announcements, Mr. Insley took attendance. There were more kids from my old school than I realized, but no Callie.

As Mr. Insley started to explain about how to get around the school, I got this crazy urge to talk to Callie. I carefully reached for my cell phone in my backpack.

I know what you're thinking: *She can't use her cell phone in class!* And you're right. I knew that. But it was like some alien or something was controlling my hands.

Must . . . text . . . Callie.

I slipped the phone under the desk and flipped

it open. I glanced at Mr. Insley and then I quickly texted my best friend.

> What happened this morning? R u taking the
> bus home or walking again?

I sent the text and looked up at Mr. Insley again. He had his back to the class, pointing to a map of the school projected on the screen. So far so good.

I felt the phone buzz in my hands and checked Callie's reply.

> Let's talk after

After what? I wondered frantically. After home-room? After school? My alien hands started texting again.

> Where r u now? Where is ur homeroom? Should
> we talk b4 class? Or I can meet u

"Miss Brown, is it?"

I looked up to see Mr. Insley standing right over me! I was so busted. I felt my face get hot.

"Um, yes," I managed to squeak out.

"I should probably remind you of the rule that there is no texting during class in this school,"

Mr. Insley said. "Normally, I'd have to confiscate your phone. But since it's the first day of school, consider this a warning."

I nodded and stuffed the phone in my backpack. I could hear kids laughing behind me.

"Bus-ted," Maggie sang in a loud whisper, then giggled.

Did you ever wish that you could blink your eyes and magically disappear? That's exactly how I felt. I'd even take a time machine—I could go back in time to the start of homeroom and leave my cell phone in my backpack. Or how about wings? I could unfurl them and fly out the window, far away from middle school.

But I was stuck with the awful reality of being humiliated in homeroom. There was nowhere to run.

Fortunately the bell rang. One good thing about being in the front row was that I could make a quick getaway. I dashed into the hallway.

Crowds of kids streamed through the halls. Callie had to be somewhere close by, right? I walked up and down, trying to find her.

Then I noticed that kids were opening their lockers and putting their backpacks inside. I had a feeling I was supposed to be doing that too. *Where was that schedule again? It had to be here somewhere. . . . Found it!*

I took it out and tried to find my locker on the map that was on the bottom of my schedule. I had locker number 213. Isn't thirteen supposed to be an unlucky number? But, luckily, it was just down the hallway.

The locker had a built-in lock. I spun the dial, searching for the combination numbers that were printed on my schedule.

26 . . . 14 . . . 5 . . .

The door wouldn't open the first time. The hallway was getting emptier by the second. Panic started to well up inside me.

I took a deep breath and tried again.

26 . . . 14 . . . 5 . . . Click!

The door popped open, and I shoved my backpack inside. I took out the notebook I needed for my next class, science.

I slammed the locker shut and checked the schedule again. Science was in room 234, on the left leg of the *U*. It should have been easy to find, except I wasn't sure what part of the *U* I was in.

I guess if I had been paying attention to Mr. Insley, I would have known where to go. I ran down the hall as fast as I could and turned the corner. Room 234 should have been the first door on the right.

I stepped in the doorway, breathless. I looked around for a seat.

That's when I noticed the chalkboard.

French—Bonjour!

Mademoiselle Girard

I was in the wrong room!

A girl with reddish hair in the front row saw me. "You look lost," she said.

"I am," I told her. "I'm trying to find science. Room 234."

She pointed to the doorway with her pencil. "Right across the hall," she said.

"Thanks!"

I raced across the hallway just as the bell rang.

I was going to be late for my very first class! Could this day get any worse?

CHAPTER 4

Abandoned at Lunch

Okay, so it turned out that I wasn't the only one who was late, and we weren't in any trouble. The science teacher, Ms. Biddle, waved us all in.

"Enter, enter, all you lost souls," she said.

I liked Ms. Biddle right away. She wasn't much taller than any of us students, and her blond hair was spiked on top of her head. She wore a bright blue T-shirt that said EVIL MUTANT SCIENCE TEACHER.

"Welcome to science," she announced. "I am Ms. Biddle, and this is my co-teacher, Priscilla."

She pointed to a plastic skeleton hanging from a stand in the front corner of the room. A bunch of us laughed.

"Based on the existence of Priscilla in this class-room, who can create a hypothesis about what we're going to learn this semester?" she asked.

I raised my hand. "The human body?"

"Excellent!" the teacher cheered. "What a bright bunch of students. I can tell this is going to be a great year."

My humiliating homeroom experience took a backseat in my brain. I really had fun in science class. Science has always been my favorite subject. And I had a feeling that Ms. Biddle could make any subject fun, even math.

When science ended, I resisted the urge to look for Callie in the hallway. I didn't want to be late again. My next class was social studies with Mr. Insley, back in homeroom.

I stopped at my locker and got my social studies notebook on the first try. I made it to the room before the bell rang.

"Hey, it's the cell phone girl," Mr. Insley said when he saw me, and I cringed a little. But I recovered quickly.

"Cell phone? What cell phone?" I joked, and to my relief, he gave me a smile.

Social studies went pretty smoothly too—but still no Callie.

I knew my next period was lunch, and I felt sure I would see her there. I had to. If I didn't talk with her soon, I knew I would go crazy!

I had to stop back at my locker to get my lunch. I swiftly spun the dial.

26 . . . 15 . . . 14.

Nothing happened.

"Okay," I told my locker. "We can do this the hard way or the easy way."

I tried the combination again, and it still didn't work. Frustrated, I pulled my schedule out of my notebook and checked it again.

26 . . . 14 . . . 5. I'd gotten the numbers mixed up.

"Sorry," I told my locker. "My bad."

I grabbed my lunch and raced to the cafeteria but, of course, I was one of the last people to get there.

The cafeteria was twice as big as the one in my old school. Kids sat at rectangular tables that stretched all the way to the back of the room. More kids were lined up in front of the steaming lunch counter along the wall to my right.

It didn't take me long to spot Callie in the crowd. She was sitting at a table with Sydney, Maggie, and Brenda.

Somehow I wasn't surprised. But I wasn't exactly prepared either. What was I supposed to do? Just walk up and sit with them?

Why not? I asked myself. *You and Callie have sat together at lunch every day for years. Why should today be any different?*

I took a deep breath and walked toward the table. There was an empty seat. Perfect!

"Hi," I said, moving toward the seat. But Sydney stopped me with just a few words.

"Sorry, Katie," she said. "This table is reserved for the PGC."

"What's the PGC?" I asked.

"Popular. Girls. Club," Sydney replied, saying each word slowly, to make sure I understood. "You have to be a member to sit here. And you are not."

I turned to Callie. "So, you're a member?"

"Yeah," she said. "It's no big deal, Katie, it's just—"

"Right. No big deal," I said quickly. I didn't want to hear what Callie had to say. I just needed to get away from that table. I felt like I couldn't breathe.

"Hey, Katie!" I heard Callie call behind me. "I'll call you later!"

I walked away and tried to find another seat. I could feel tears forming in my eyes. I could *not* cry in the middle of the cafeteria on my first day of school. I just couldn't.

I saw some kids from Hamilton at other tables, but I walked right past them. I headed for an empty table in the back of the room and sat down.

What had just happened? Callie had joined a club, and I wasn't invited. Fine. But couldn't she at least have warned me before today?

I opened my lunch bag. I didn't feel much like eating, but Mom would be disappointed if I didn't at least try the special lunch she made for me.

Mom had packed carrot sticks with ranch dip (my favorite) and a tuna fish sandwich, plus my aluminum water bottle filled with apple juice. Besides all that, there was a pink plastic cupcake holder, the kind that's shaped exactly like a cupcake. Mom had written on it with a glitter marker, "A cupcake for my Cupcake." Corny, yes, but I knew the cupcake inside would be delicious.

Suddenly I realized I was hungry after all. I unwrapped the sandwich and took a bite.

"Is anyone sitting here?"

I looked up to see Mia, the girl from the bus.

"No, unless they're invisible," I replied. Mia smiled and sat in the chair across from me.

"How's everything going so far?" Mia asked me. She was opening up her lunch bag and taking out a container of what looked like vegetable sushi rolls.

"Let's see," I began. "I got in trouble in homeroom for using my cell phone. My locker hates me.

I keep getting lost. And, oh yeah, my best friend would rather hang out with a bunch of mean girls than me."

Mia raised an eyebrow. "Really?"

"It's all true," I said solemnly. "How about you?"

Mia shrugged. "It's okay . . . just, different. Hey, did you have science yet? Isn't Ms. Biddle awesome?"

I nodded. "I know! I love her T-shirt."

As we were talking, two girls approached our table, carrying trays of food. I recognized one of them as the girl with the reddish hair who helped me find the science room.

"Hi," I said. "Do you want to sit down? There's plenty of room."

"Thanks," said the girl I recognized.

"I'm Mia," Mia said.

"And I'm Katie," I added.

"Hi. I'm Alexis," she replied. "And this is Emma."

"Hi," Emma said shyly.

Alexis's reddish hair was neatly pulled back in a white headband that matched her white button-down shirt. She wore a short denim skirt and ballet flats. I noticed everything matched.

Emma had big blue eyes and straight blond hair. She was really pretty. She had on a sleeveless pink dress with small white flowers on it and white sneakers.

"Did you guys go to Richardson?" I guessed.

Alexis nodded. "Right. Did you go to Hamilton?"

"I did," I replied. "But Mia's from Manhattan."

"Ooh, I always wanted to go there," Emma said. "I heard there's a museum with a giant whale that hangs from the ceiling, and you can walk right underneath it. Have you ever been there?"

Mia nodded. "It's so cool. It's amazing to imagine that something that big lives on the planet, you know?" she said. "You should go sometime. Manhattan's not that far from here."

"Maybe someday," Emma said wistfully.

"So has anyone had that math teacher yet, Mrs. Moore?" Mia asked. She shuddered. "Scary."

"Uh-oh," I said. "I have her next period."

"Me too. But I heard she's not so bad," Alexis told us. "My sister Dylan told me she's strict, but if you just do what she says, you'll be all right."

I finished my sandwich and dug into my carrot sticks. Mia, Alexis, and Emma were really nice, but I couldn't stop thinking about Callie. I glanced over at the PGC table. Callie was laughing at something Sydney was saying. Were they laughing about me?

I didn't realize it at first, but I was accidentally

ignoring the girls at the table, so I quickly tuned back in.

"Earth to Katie," Alexis said. "I was asking you if you had social studies yet."

"Oh, sorry," I said.

"Her best friend dumped her to hang out with some mean girls," Mia explained.

"Really?" Alexis asked. "Which ones?"

I pointed to Sydney's table.

"Oh, I know those girls from camp," she said, shaking her head. "You're right. They are mean. Especially that Sydney."

"I don't know what Callie's doing with them," I said with a sigh.

"Callie?" Alexis said. "I know her from camp too. She always seemed nice."

I reached into my lunch bag and took out my cupcake holder. For a second I forgot about the corny message my mom had decorated it with. I tried to turn it around so the other girls wouldn't see it, but it was too late.

"Aw, that's cute," Mia said.

"Thanks," I replied, relieved. I opened the cupcake holder and took out the sweet treasure inside.

"Wow, your mom packed you a cupcake?" Emma asked. "Lucky!"

The icing was a light brown color. I sniffed it.

"Peanut butter," I said out loud. "With cinnamon."

"What's inside?" Emma asked.

I took a bite, and a yummy glob of grape jelly squirted into my mouth.

"Jelly," I reported. "It's a P-B-and-J cupcake."

I took another bite, making sure to get the icing and the jelly in the bite at the same time. Like all of mom's cupcakes, it was superdelicious.

At least some things never change, I thought.

I realized that all of the girls were eyeing me a little bit enviously. I couldn't blame them. I mean, who doesn't like cupcakes?

"I've never heard of a peanut-butter-and-jelly cupcake before," Emma said.

"There's a cupcake shop in my dad's neighborhood that has fifty-seven flavors," Mia told us. "I bet they have P-B-and-J."

I thought about offering them a bite, but I already had my germs all over it, and the jelly was getting kind of messy.

"The next time my mom makes cupcakes, I'll bring some for all of us," I promised.

"Cool," Mia said.

"Thanks," said Alexis and Emma at the same time.

The lunch bell rang. It was time for my next class.

I stuffed my empty cupcake holder into my bag. My first day of middle school wasn't even half over, but I had a feeling that the only good part of it had just ended.

CHAPTER 5

The Cupcake Cure

So here's what happened the rest of the day:

- Forgot my locker combination after lunch.
- Was late to math class. Mrs. Moore gave me a sheet of math problems to do as punishment. Mia was right! She *is* scary.
- No gym until next week, so I hung out with Emma, who's in my gym class. (Okay, something went right.)
- Had English with Mia, Alexis, and Emma. Good. But left my summer reading report in my locker. Bad!
- Had art as my special class for seventh period. Found out that there's cooking, but I can't take that until January. Rats!

• Spanish is my last class of the day. Then it's *adios*!
• No Callie in *any* of my classes.

When the last bell rang, I stuffed all of my books into my backpack and went outside to look for Joanne's car.

Joanne works in my mom's office. When I was in elementary school, I went to an after-school program until Mom got off of work. But there's no after-school program for middle school. Mom doesn't think I'm old enough to go home by myself. So her plan was for me to hang out at the office every day. Doesn't that sound like fun?

Anyway, she told me Joanne had a small red car, so I started looking around for it. Then I heard Sydney's voice behind me.

"Looking for your former friend?"

I turned and saw Sydney, with Maggie and Brenda laughing behind her. At least Callie wasn't with them. I turned around without answering.

Then I heard a beep. Joanne was waving out of a car window down by the parking lot. I ran to meet her.

"Hey, Katie. How was your first day of middle school? Was it awesome?" Joanne asked.

"Sure," I said, sliding into the front seat.

I like Joanne a lot. She's really tall and has lots of blond hair that she piles on top of her head. She always talks to me like I'm a person, not a little kid. Not all adults know how to do that.

"Hmm. You don't sound so sure," Joanne said.

"It was fine," I told her.

I really didn't feel like talking about it. Not just now, anyway. Sydney had put me in a really bad mood.

Joanne seemed to understand.

"Cool," she said. "Your mom's been talking about you all day. She can't wait to see you."

When we got to the office, my mom was busy with a patient. Joanne set me up in my mom's personal office, where she has a desk and a phone and all of her books about dentist stuff.

"Gotta go," Joanne said. "Yell if you need me. But not too loud. Don't want to scare the patients."

"Thanks!" I told her.

Then I took out my cell phone and called Callie. The phone rang three times before she picked up.

"Hello?"

"Cal, it's Katie. Can you talk?" I asked.

"Of course," Callie answered, and for a second I wondered if the whole day had been some kind of weird dream. Callie sounded like she always did.

"Why didn't you tell me we weren't taking the bus together?" I blurted out.

"Listen, Katie, I'm sorry," Callie said, and she sounded like she meant it. "I became good friends with Sydney, Maggie, and Bella at camp. And they asked me to join their club. I wanted to tell you, but we never got together."

"Okay, but—wait, Bella? I thought her name was Brenda?" I asked.

"It was, but she changed it to Bella," Callie explained.

"Oh," I said. I'd never known anyone who actually changed his or her name before. But that wasn't important right now. "You could have called me. Or texted me," I said.

"I know, I know, but I was really busy when I got back. Honest," Callie said. "Please don't be upset."

"Are we still friends?" I asked. There was a lump in my throat when I said the word.

"Of course!" Callie assured me. "You're my best friend."

"But you won't walk to school with me or have lunch with me," I pointed out. I knew I sounded like a baby, and I really was about to cry. I was just so confused.

"It's not like that," Callie protested. "Katie, we're

in middle school now. Middle school is bigger than just the two of us. We're going to make lots of new friends. Both of us."

I thought briefly about Mia, Alexis, and Emma. Callie had a point—but I was too angry and hurt to admit it.

"Sure—right," I said lamely.

"And I'll see you this weekend," Callie said. "For the annual Labor Day barbecue."

"Okay," I said with a sigh.

"Hey, did you notice I got contact lenses?" Callie asked. "No more glasses for me!" So that explained why she wasn't wearing glasses today.

"Well, I already have homework to do. Plus I need to figure out what I'm going to wear tomorrow!" Callie said, and then we hung up.

I felt better after the call—not much, but just a little. I was glad Callie was still my friend. But the whole thing was weird. Callie was basically saying, "I'm sorry, but I'm still going to ignore you at lunch tomorrow."

I've heard "I'm sorry—but . . ." a lot in my life. Mostly from my dad. As in, "I'm sorry, Katie, but I can't come visit you this summer. . . ."

It doesn't feel good.

I took out my math assignment—my only homework assignment for tonight—and started working on the problems. Just as I was finishing, Mom opened the door.

"There you are!" she said, crushing me in a hug. She smelled like mint toothpaste. "I'll be ready to go in just a few minutes, okay?"

As you can probably guess, Mom was full of questions on the car ride home.

"Are your teachers nice?"

"Did you get any homework?"

"Did you find the bus stop okay?"

"Did you like your cupcake?"

"Is Callie in any of your classes?"

That one was the hardest to answer. I couldn't bring myself to tell Mom everything that had happened with Callie. How could I, when *I* wasn't even sure what was happening?

"We only have lunch together," I replied.

"Oh, that's too bad!" Mom said with a frown. "At least you get to sit together."

I just nodded and looked out the window.

"You must be tired," Mom said. "You've had a big day today. Try to relax when we get home. I'll call you when it's time to set the table."

Because it was the first day of school, Mom made my favorite food for dinner: Chinese-style chicken and broccoli with rice. (Yes, I'm a weirdo who likes broccoli.) It smelled so good!

"Would you like to do anything after dinner?" Mom asked. "It's nice out. We could walk over to Callie's."

Not a good idea! But I didn't tell Mom that.

"I was thinking," I said. "Can we make some pineapple upside-down cupcakes?"

Mom got a knowing look on her face. "Ah. So you need a cupcake cure?"

Once, when I was seven, I fell off of my bike and messed up my knee really bad. Mom made me pineapple upside-down cupcakes and gave them to me with a note: "Turn your frown upside down." Hey, I've been telling you she's corny. Since then, we make pineapple upside-down cupcakes together whenever one of us is feeling sad. We call it the "cupcake cure." It's hard to not feel better when you eat a cupcake.

I nodded. As we took out the ingredients and started measuring, I started talking—not about Callie, but about everything else. My evil locker. Being late for class all the time. Scary Mrs. Moore.

Mom listened while I talked. When I was done, she had a bunch of suggestions for how to make things better. Mom lives to solve all of my problems. Unfortunately, I didn't tell her about my biggest problem.

Pineapple upside-down cupcakes are not that hard to make. The trick is that you don't use cupcake liners. You spray the cupcake tins with that nonstick stuff. Then you fill the bottom of each cup with a mix of canned pineapple and some spices. You pour the batter on top and then you bake them.

When the cupcakes are done, you take them out of the pan and turn them upside down. Each cupcake has a beautiful golden pineapple on the top. To make them extra nice you can add a candied cherry on top like we do.

Mom and I each ate one with a glass of milk. They were still warm. So yummy!

As Mom packed one for me in my cupcake holder, I remembered what I'd told the girls at lunch.

"Can I bring in three more?" I asked. "For the girls at my lunch table."

"Of course," Mom said. "I have a small box we can use."

I found myself looking forward to tomorrow's lunch—even without Callie.

CHAPTER 6

The Perfect Plan . . . Almost

By lunchtime the next day, I was sure of one thing.

My locker is an evil robot in disguise, sent here to Earth to prevent me from finishing middle school. Or maybe it's from the future; I'm not sure.

But I'm sure its mission is to ruin my middle school career. Maybe one day I'll become president of the United States and save the Earth from the alien or robot invasion. But if I never finish middle school, I can't become president, and the robots will rule forever.

My mom had written my combination on an orange rubber band for me to wear around my wrist so I wouldn't forget. But even with the right combination the locker wouldn't open on the first try, or even the second try! How could that be?

I was late for science again, but Ms. Biddle didn't care. I knew that Mrs. Moore was another story, though. So I devised a plan: I would take my math book with me to lunch. Then I would walk to class with Alexis, who seemed to know her way around. That way, I'd be on time.

When I finally got my locker open before lunch, I spotted the white box of cupcakes on my top shelf. I couldn't forget those! I carefully picked them up by the string, eager to show them off to the girls.

I was a little nervous, of course. What if they all decided to sit somewhere else? But when I got to the table in the back of the room, Mia was already there.

Mia's eyes got big when she saw the white box.

"Ooh, are those cupcakes?" she asked.

"My mom and I ended up making some last night," I explained.

"That's really nice of you," Mia said.

Alexis and Emma came over and dropped their books on the table.

"We've got to get in line before it gets too long," Alexis said.

"Hurry back," Mia said. "Katie brought cupcakes."

Emma flashed me a grateful smile as she and Alexis headed off to the lunch line.

Soon we were all eating lunch together. Mom had packed me some leftover chicken and broccoli, which tastes even better cold.

"I can't believe it's Friday already!" Alexis said. "It's weird, starting school and then having three days off."

"I think they're trying to ease us into it—you know, like how you stick only your foot in a pool when it's really cold, and then slowly put the rest of your body in," I guessed.

"I always jump right in," Emma said. "Cold or not."

Mia shuddered. "You're brave!"

"I think we're going to the beach this weekend," Alexis said. "Last swim of the summer."

"I'm going to the city this weekend, to see my dad," Mia chimed in.

"Are your parents divorced?" Alexis asked, like it was no big deal.

Mia nodded. "Four years ago."

I didn't say anything about my own parents being divorced. To be honest, I was a little jealous that Mia was going to see her dad. I hadn't seen mine in years.

"We're going to my grandma's house for a picnic," Emma spoke up.

"We're going to a barbecue," I said. "Over at . . . Callie's."

I glanced over at the PGC table.

"Isn't that the friend who dumped you?" Alexis asked.

"She didn't dump me," I protested. "We're still friends. Best friends."

"Emma is my best friend," Alexis said. "If she sat at a table with other girls, I'd sit next to her."

"But I wouldn't sit at a table with other girls," Emma said, and then she gave me an apologetic look, like she was worried she'd hurt my feelings.

"Exactly," said Alexis. They both looked at me.

"Look, it's kind of complicated," I said. "They formed this club. The Popular Girls Club. And you can't sit at the table unless you're a member. It's a rule."

"Are you serious? They actually named themselves the Popular Girls Club?" Alexis asked. "If you're popular, do you really have to advertise it like that? Plus, what did everyone do—take a vote or something?"

Mia had an amused smile on her face. "It does seem a little desperate," she admitted. "But I have all

43

of those girls in a lot of my classes. They seem nice."

"Callie is nice," I said. "Really. I'm just not so sure about the others."

There was a weird silence.

"So, Katie." Mia nodded to the white box. "When do we get to try those cupcakes?"

"Right now," I answered. I slipped off the string and opened up the top of the box. The cupcakes looked perfect.

"They're so pretty!" Emma cooed.

"What is that golden stuff?" Alexis asked.

"It's pineapple," I explained. "These are like pineapple upside-down cake, except they're cup-cakes."

Mia shook her head. "Where do you get all these amazing cupcake ideas?"

"It's my mom, mostly," I admitted. "She's cup-cake crazy."

Mia laughed. "My mom is shopping crazy."

"You're lucky," said Alexis. "My mom is cleaning crazy."

Emma shrugged. "My mom says me and my brothers make *her* crazy."

"She has three brothers," Alexis told us. "They're all monsters. Emma is the only normal one."

Emma blushed.

"Less talking, more cupcakes," I joked, and each of us picked one up.

It was quiet for a second as we took a bite of golden goodness.

"These are absolutely delicious," Mia said.

Alexis nodded. "The pineapple is supergood."

"I love the cherry on top," Emma said.

I was happy that everyone liked them.

"I'll bring in cupcakes every day if I can," I offered.

"That might be cupcake overload," Alexis pointed out. "Even for your cupcake crazy mother. How about one day a week? Like every Friday?"

"Cupcake Friday," I said. "I like it."

I liked it for a bunch of reasons. Making cupcakes is fun. But it also meant my new friends wanted to sit with me—for at least another week.

The bell rang, and I turned to Alexis. "Can I follow you to math? I don't want to be late."

"Of course!" Alexis replied.

We got to math in plenty of time. Mrs. Moore was already there.

"How nice to see you on time, Miss Brown," Mrs. Moore told me.

I felt fantastic. My plan had worked.

When the bell rang, Mrs. Moore asked us all to

take out our math books. I looked down at my desk. I had my notebook with me, but not my math book! Had I left it at lunch?

Then I remembered. I had grabbed the cupcake box instead of my math book! It was still in my locker.

With a sigh, I raised my hand. "Excuse me, Mrs. Moore . . ."

She gave me *two* worksheets that night!

CHAPTER 7

Just Like Old Times . . . Almost

The morning of Labor Day I woke up with a huge knot in my stomach. I didn't know what it would be like with Callie at the barbecue. And this year I wanted everything to be especially perfect.

Unfortunately, my need for perfection made me argue with my mom about what kind of decorations to put on the cupcakes we were bringing. The night before, we made vanilla cupcakes with vanilla icing, which are Callie's dad's favorite. That's a pretty boring cupcake, so we always add some decoration on the top. Sometimes it's candy. But lately, Mom's been into using this stuff called fondant. It's like a kind of dough, but it's mostly made out of sugar. You can color it, roll it out, and cut shapes out of it just like cookie dough. But you don't have to cook it. Then you can put the shapes on top of your cupcakes and they look amazing. It's a little hard to make, but as I said, Mom is like Martha Stewart. She could make a house out of fondant if she had to.

Mom and I were looking through the tin of mini cookie cutters for shapes to use. I wanted to use a sun and color the fondant yellow. Mom wanted to use a leaf shape and color the fondant orange.

"But it's still summer," I whined. "It's, like, a hundred degrees out there."

"Eighty-five," Mom corrected me. "And summer is over. School's started."

"But the first day of autumn isn't until September twenty-third," I said. "That's a fact. A scientific fact."

"Technically," Mom agreed. "But as soon as I see school buses driving around, I think of fall."

I frowned. I didn't want summer to end just yet. Mom looked at me. She knew something was wrong and I didn't want to tell her what it was. I sighed and gave in.

"How about half suns and half leaves?" I suggested.

Mom smiled. "Perfect! The orange and yellow will look nice together."

By noon we were pulling into the driveway of

Callie's house. It's easy to find because it's the only house on the block painted light blue. From the sidewalk you can tell which room is Callie's—it's the window on the second floor on the left with the unicorn decal on it. I have one just like it on my bedroom window.

We walked through the white wood gate and headed right for the backyard. Callie's dad was standing by the grill on the deck.

"Hey, Katie-did!" he called out. He wiggled his eyebrows when he saw the cupcake holder in my arms. "I hope that is filled with lots of vanilla cupcakes!"

"Of course!" I replied. "With vanilla icing."

Mr. Wilson gave me and my mom a hug. He's got kind of a big belly, so his hugs are always squishy.

"It's Barbara's fault. All that good cooking," he'll say, patting his stomach, and everybody always laughs.

I've known Mr. Wilson—and Callie's whole family—since even before I was born. My mom and Callie's mom met in a cooking class while they were pregnant. In a way, the Wilsons are like my second family. Mrs. Wilson is like my second mom. Callie's like a sister. And Mr. Wilson's like a dad. And since I never see my dad, he's the closest thing to one that I've got.

Then it hit me as I was standing there on the deck. If Callie and I stopped being friends, what would happen to my whole second family?

I didn't have much time to think about it because Callie and her mom came out onto the deck. Callie's mom and my mom gave each other a big hug. Callie and I nodded to each other. Things definitely felt a little weird between us.

"Where's Jenna today?" Mom asked. Jenna is Callie's older sister. She's a junior in high school. Callie has an older brother, too, named Stephen. He just started college this year.

"She's with her *friends*," Mrs. Wilson said, rolling her eyes. "When you're sixteen, a family barbecue is apparently a horrible punishment."

Mom looked at me and Callie. "Well, we've got a few more years left with these two, don't we?"

I hate when parents talk like that. Like when we're teenagers we're going to turn into hideous mutants or something. It kind of made me nervous, in a way. What if they were right?

"So how do you like middle school, Katie?" Callie's mom asked me.

I shrugged. "It's only been two days. It's kind of hard to tell."

"I'm so glad the girls are on the same bus route,"

my mom said. "Middle school can be pretty scary. It's nice that they have each other to navigate through it."

Mrs. Wilson looked confused. "Callie told me she's been walking to school. Aren't you two walking together?"

Callie looked down at her flip-flops.

"It's no big deal," I said quickly. "I like to take the bus. Callie likes to walk."

I just didn't want to get into a whole big discussion about it. Not in front of our mothers, anyway. I saw Mom biting her bottom lip. She looked at Callie's mom and raised her eyebrows.

"Callie, why didn't you mention this?" her mom asked.

Before Callie could answer, Mr. Wilson stepped into our circle.

"Hey, it's going to be about a half hour before the food is ready," he said. "I inflated the volleyball this morning. How about a game of moms against kids?"

That sounded good to me. I'm terrible at volleyball, but I still think it's fun. Besides, anything would be better than standing around talking about why Callie and I weren't taking the bus together.

"Kids serve first!" I yelled, and I ran into the yard

and grabbed the ball. I tossed it to Callie. "You'd better start. You know I usually can't get it over the net."

Callie laughed, and we launched into the game. Let me explain what happens when I play volleyball: I will chase after any ball that comes over the net. I will hit it with everything I've got. The problem is I have no idea how to aim it. Sometimes the ball goes way off to the side. Sometimes it goes behind me, over my head. If I'm lucky, it'll go right over the net. But that doesn't happen a lot.

Pretty soon Callie and I were cracking up laughing. We kept bumping into each other, and once we both tumbled onto the grass. It was really hilarious. And the funniest thing is that even though I am terrible at the game, we still beat the moms!

"That's game! Katie and Callie win!" Mr. Wilson called up from the deck.

"Woo-hoo!" Callie and I cried, high-fiving each other.

"And that's perfect timing," Callie's dad added. "Lunch is ready!"

Mr. Wilson might blame Callie's mom for his big stomach, but he is a great cook too. After I drank two big glasses of lemonade (volleyball makes me thirsty) I dug in to the food on the table. There were hamburgers, hot dogs, potato salad, juicy tomatoes from the garden, and of course, corn on the cob. I put a piece of corn on my plate before anything else.

"Katie, remember the time you ate six pieces of corn on the cob?" Callie asked, giggling.

"I was only six!" I cried.

"I can't believe we weren't paying attention," my mom said, shaking her head. "Six pieces. Can you imagine that?"

"And I didn't even get a stomachache," I said proudly.

"I love corn on the cob, but I could never eat six pieces," Callie added.

The rest of lunch was like that. We told funny stories, and we laughed a lot. It was just like last year's Labor Day barbecue. Like nothing at all had changed.

"Want to go to my room?" Callie asked when we were done.

"Sure," I said.

"I might eat all the cupcakes while you're gone!" Mr. Wilson warned.

I hadn't been in Callie's room in more than a month. Some things were the same, like the unicorn decal and her purple walls and carpet. And the picture of me and Callie from when we went to an amusement park and had our faces painted like tigers. Callie with her blond hair and blue eyes, me with my brown hair and brown eyes. Totally different—but the tiger paint made us look like sisters.

Other stuff was new. Like now she had lots of posters on her walls—lots of posters of boys. Most of them were from those vampire movies.

When did she start liking those? I wondered.

"You've got to see my pictures from camp," Callie said. "I have so much to tell you."

"I know," I said. "This is, like, the first time we've been together."

Callie held up her cell phone so I could see it and started scrolling through the photos. As they whizzed by, I saw lots of pictures of her and Sydney and the others. She stopped at a photo of a boy on a diving board.

"That's Matt," she said. "Isn't he cute? He was a lifeguard at camp."

I squinted at the photo. Matt had short brown hair and he was wearing a red bathing suit. He looked like a regular boy to me. But he didn't have tentacles or antennae or a tail or anything, so I guessed that was a good sign.

"He's in eighth grade," Callie said. "I pass him in the hallway every day between fifth and sixth period. The other day he actually said, 'Hi, Callie.' Isn't that amazing?"

Wow, he can put two words together, I thought. But out loud I said, "Yeah, amazing."

Callie's cell phone made a sound like fairy bells. The photo faded and a text message popped up on the screen.

"No way!" she cried. "*Teen Style* magazine has posted the best and worst fashion from the music awards last night. You have got to check this out!"

It was easy to guess who the text message was from—Sydney. It had to be.

Callie grabbed her laptop and started typing away. A page popped up on the screen.

"That's hilarious," she said. "They divided the page into 'Killer Looks' and 'Looks That Should Be Killed.' Ha!"

I briefly wondered what kind of weapon would be used to kill an ugly dress. Maybe some robo-scissors?

"Oh my gosh, that is *awful!*" Callie squealed. She grabbed her cell phone and started texting.

Any fuzzy feelings I'd had before were evaporating. Callie was supposed to be hanging out with me today. It was like I wasn't even in the room.

"Hey, Callie," I said.

"Yeah?" She looked up from her phone.

"I know we're still friends," I said. "But the other day you said we were still best friends. I'm just wondering about that. I mean . . . *best* friends sit together at lunch. They talk to each other during school."

"I know," Callie said. "But it's complicated. I still wish we could be best friends, but . . ." She sighed and looked away.

That's the moment I knew there was no going back. Callie had changed over the summer.

"But what?" I asked.

"You're still my friend, Katie. You'll always be my friend."

"Just not best friends," I said quietly.

Callie didn't answer, but she didn't have to.

"I don't under—"

Then I heard my mom's voice in the doorway. "Girls, it's cupcake time."

Mom had a kind of sad look on her face. I wondered how long she'd been standing there.

I figured Mom would be full of questions on the ride home. But for once, she wasn't. I stared out the window, thinking.

Tomorrow I'd start my first full week of school. There would be no more barbecues. No more swimming. Just day after day of middle school.

Maybe Mom was right. It wasn't September twenty-third yet, but summer was officially over.

CHAPTER 8

Just Call Me "Silly Arms"

*T*uesday wasn't just the start of my first real week of school. It was also the first day of gym.

I knew gym was going to be different from how it was in elementary school. For one thing, we have to wear a gym uniform: blue shorts and a blue T-shirt that says PARK STREET MIDDLE SCHOOL in yellow writing on it. I wasn't too worried about the changing-into-the-uniform thing. I just put my favorite unicorn underwear in a different drawer so I won't accidentally wear it during the week. Nobody needs to know about my unicorn underwear.

I also knew that the gym would be bigger, and the teachers would be different. But what I didn't count on was that the kids in gym would be different too. I'm not just talking about the kids from other schools. Kids I've known all my life had completely changed. Like Eddie Rossi, for example. Somehow he grew a mustache over the summer. An actual mustache! And Ken Watanabe—he must have grown a whole foot taller.

The boys were all rowdier, too. Before class started they were running around, wrestling, and slamming into one another like they were Ultimate Fighting Champs or something. I moved closer to Emma for safety.

"They're gonna hurt somebody," I said, worried.

Emma shrugged. I guess having three brothers, she's used to it.

Our gym teacher's name is Kelly Chen. She looks like someone you'd see in a commercial for a sports drink. Her shiny black hair is always in a perfect ponytail, and she wears a neat blue sweat suit with yellow stripes down the sides.

She blew a whistle to start the class.

"Line up in rows for me, people!" she called out. "We don't do anything in this class without warming up."

We did a bunch of stretches and things to get started. That was easy enough. Then Ms. Chen divided us into four teams to play volleyball.

You can probably see what's coming. I didn't—not right away. We always played volleyball in elementary school. Everybody had fun, and most kids were pretty terrible at it, just like me. So I wasn't too worried.

My first warning should have been when I got my team assignment. Ms. Chen put me on a team with Sydney and Maggie! Ken Watanabe was on our team too, along with two boys I didn't know named Wes and Aziz.

On the other team were a bunch of kids I didn't know and George Martinez from my old school. Emma was on a team playing on the other side of the gym, so George was the only friendly face in sight.

"All right, take your places!" Ms. Chen called out.

Everyone scrambled to get in line. For some reason, I was in place to serve the first ball. Ken tossed it to me.

My hands were starting to sweat a little.

"What are you waiting for?" Sydney called out.

I took a deep breath and punched the ball with my right hand.

It soared up . . . up . . . and wildly to the right, slamming into the bleachers. It bounced off and then bounced into the basketball pole, ricocheting like a pinball in a machine. Then it rolled to Ms. Chen's feet. She tossed it to the other team.

"Nice serve," Sydney said snidely, and Maggie giggled next to her.

My face flushed red. The only good thing about messing up the serve was that I got to move out of serving position. I wouldn't have to serve again for a while.

I was safe while I was in the back row. Ken was in front, and he was so tall that no ball could get past him. The other kids were all hitting the ball pretty well too. It was like everyone had suddenly become volleyball experts over the summer. Why hadn't I acquired this amazing skill?

But then it was time for us to switch positions, and I was in front of the net. My hands started to sweat again.

Sydney served the ball, and George volleyed it back. It was one of those balls that kisses the top of the net and then slowly drops over, like a gift. It should have been easy to hit.

Not for me. I swung my arm underhand to get to it, and the ball went flying behind me. Aziz tried to get it but it bounced out of bounds.

George was grinning. "Katie, you look like that

sprinkler in my backyard, you know, Silly Arms? The one with all those arms and they wave around and sprinkle water everywhere?"

George started spinning around and waving his arms in a weird, wiggly way. Everyone started laughing.

I was laughing too. George and I have been teasing each other since kindergarten. I knew he wasn't trying to hurt my feelings.

But then Sydney and Maggie had to take the fun out of it.

"Do you guys want Silly Arms on your team? We'll trade you," Sydney called out.

"Yeah, we'll never win with this one on our team," Maggie added.

I couldn't wait for gym to be over. For the rest of the game, George wiggled his arms like the Silly Arms sprinkler every time the ball came to him. If I wasn't so mad at Sydney and Maggie, I would have thought it was funny. Instead, I was miserable. As soon as I got back to the locker room I changed fast and ran out.

I had English class next. It's the one class I have with Mia, Emma, and Alexis. George Martinez is in that class too. He walked past me on the way to his seat.

"Hey, Silly Arms," he said with a grin.

"What's that about?" Mia asked.

"Gym class," I said with a sigh. "We were playing volleyball, and George said my arms look like the Silly Arms sprinkler."

"That's so mean!" Mia said.

"But it's true," I told her. "I think I hate gym now."

"Tell me about it." Mia rolled her eyes. "Gym was so much better in my old school. We got to bring in our iPods and dance to the music we brought in."

I noticed that Mia was wearing another model-worthy outfit: a belted gray sweater vest over a blue-and-black striped T-shirt dress, tights, and short black boots with heels. That gave me an idea.

"Hey, do you know anything about the *Teen Style* website?" I asked her.

Mia's eyes lit up. "Of course! They are the best with all the new fashion trends. Why?"

"Just wondering," I said. Honestly, though, I was thinking that if I knew more about it, maybe Callie and I would have something to talk about some-time.

"I know," Mia said. "Why don't you take the bus home with me today? We can check out the web-site at my house."

The bell rang. "I'll text my mom and let you know," I whispered as Mrs. Castillo took her place in front of the room to begin today's class.

I know what you're thinking, but I did *not* text my mom in class. I had learned my lesson in homeroom. I waited until the bell rang and texted her before my next class.

Can I go to my friend Mia's after school?

The answer came back quickly. My mom may be an adult, but she is a superfast texter.

Not until I talk to Mia's parents. And what are you doing texting during school? I will take your cell phone privileges away next time.

See? Even when I try to do the right thing, I get in trouble.

I knew there was no point in replying, or I'd lose my phone. Mom is pretty strict that way.

It's not fair. I fumed as I stomped down the hall. I lost my best friend. How was I supposed to make new ones if my mom wouldn't let me?

CHAPTER 9

Teen Style and Two Tiny Dogs

I was embarrassed to tell Mia that I couldn't go until our mothers met, but she was cool about it. She quickly took my phone from me.

"Hey, why fight it?" She laughed. "My mom is the same way. I'll enter my number in your address book," she said. "Your mom can call me tonight, and I'll put my mom on the phone. Maybe we can do it tomorrow. Don't stress it."

I really admire the way Mia handles things. She's pretty cool about everything. *And* she's down to earth, too. She's totally not snobby or anything. I realized how much I liked Mia. I was starting to feel really glad that her mom had moved to our town.

So that night, I decided to play it cool, like Mia would. I gave Mia's number to Mom and told her I wanted to go the next day after school. I didn't give her a hard time about not letting me go. I couldn't resist arguing about the cell phone, though.

"You know, texting between classes doesn't count," I said.

"It's still in school," Mom countered. "And your cell phone is for emergencies *only* while you're in school, whether you're between classes or not."

It's very hard to win an argument with Mom.

But the good news is that she talked to Mia's mom, Ms. Vélaz, and they both said it was okay for me to take the bus to Mia's house after school. My mom agreed to pick me up on her way home from work. She was laughing on the phone with Mia's mom, so I figured she liked her. That was a good sign.

I was pretty excited to go to Mia's house the next day. Even gym couldn't bring me down. Ms. Chen mixed up our teams, so I didn't get stuck with Sydney and Maggie again. Even better. But I did get stuck with George, who kept calling me Silly Arms even though I was on *his* team this time. Go figure.

Mia's house was one of the last houses on the bus stop route. That's because it's in the part of town where the houses are really big and far apart. The bus stopped in front of a white house with a perfect green lawn in front. The lawn at our house is usually filled with dandelions, but Mom and I think they're pretty so we let them grow.

Mia let us in through the front door, and the first thing I noticed was the noise. Loud heavy-metal music was blasting through the whole house. Two tiny white dogs were barking on top of it. They ran up to Mia and me and started sniffing my sneakers.

"That's Milkshake and Tiki," Mia told me. "If you don't like dogs, I can put them in their crate."

"No, I love dogs!" I said. "I want one so bad, but Mom's allergic. Can I pet them?"

"Sure," she replied. I reached down to touch them, but the skittish dogs wouldn't stand still. I could barely feel the fur under my fingers.

"Follow me," Mia instructed. We went down a hallway and through one of the doors there.

A woman with black hair like Mia's and headphones on was sitting at a desk, typing on a computer.

"Mom, can you please tell Dan to turn down the music?!" Mia yelled.

But Ms. Vélaz didn't see or hear us. Mia walked over and took the headphones off her mother's ears. Ms. Vélaz smiled.

"Oh hello, Mia." She nodded to me. "And this must be Katie."

"Nice to meet you," I said.

"Mom, can you *please* tell Dan to turn down the music?" Mia pleaded.

"Would you mind asking him yourself?" her mom asked. "I'm IM'ing a potential client, and I can't leave the computer right now."

Mia sighed. "All right. But I bet he won't do it."

"Please get a snack for Katie too!" Ms. Vélaz called out to us.

We left the office, and Mia grabbed a bag of cookies before we headed up the gleaming wood staircase. Mia told me her story as best as she could over the loud music.

"Mom used to work at a fashion magazine in New York, but then she met Eddie, who already had a house out here," she explained. "So now she works out of the house. She's starting her own consulting business."

We stopped in front of a door on the second floor.

"This is Dan's room," Mia shouted. "He'll be my stepbrother when Mom and Eddie get married in a few months."

Mia pounded on the door. It slowly opened, and

a teenage boy with dark hair hanging over his eyes stood behind it.

"Too loud?" he asked.

"What do you think?" Mia shouted back.

Dan closed the door and a few seconds later the music was much quieter. Mia shook her head as we walked to her room.

"He's a junior in high school," she said. "Two more years and he's out of here. I hope."

I wondered if he knew Callie's sister, Jenna. Callie was always popping up in my head.

We stepped into Mia's room. I was kind of expecting it to be as neat and stylish as Mia. The rest of her house looked like something from a magazine. But her room was a little messy, which was fine, just kind of a surprise.

"My old room in Manhattan was *so* much nicer," she said, pointing to the wallpaper. "Can you believe those flowers? I think some old lady must have lived in here before. Eddie keeps promising that we'll paint it, but he and Mom are always so busy."

I forgot who Eddie was for a minute until I realized Mia was talking about her almost-stepdad. I have never called an adult by their first name before, except for Joanne at my mom's office, but she's not like a real adult anyway. I tried to imagine calling my mom by her first name, Sharon. Weird!

Mia pushed aside some clothes on the bed and opened up her laptop. "You want to check out *Teen Style*?" she asked.

"Sure."

"It's pretty fun," Mia said as she typed away. "They have a whole section of celebrities, and you can rate the outfits they're wearing."

She clicked a few times, and a photo of a thin, blond actress came on the screen. She was wearing a red dress with feathers on the bottom.

"What do you think?" Mia asked me.

I shrugged. "It's nice, I guess. I mean, if she likes it, then what's the difference?"

"I think it's too long," Mia said. "Take a few inches off of it and it would be perfect." She clicked on the number "7" and then a new picture popped up.

I really didn't get it. I had no idea why one outfit was better than another. But Mia had a definite opinion about everything.

We did that for a while, and then Mia clicked on another page. "This is *really* fun," she said. "You create an avatar of yourself and then you get to try on different outfits to see how they would look."

Mia made my avatar: skinny, medium height,

wavy brown hair, brown eyes. Then she started clicking on clothes, and they appeared on my avatar's body.

I couldn't tell what was wrong with other people's clothes, but it was cool to experiment and see what different stuff looked good on computer me. I had to admit that part was pretty fun. Well, for a while. Then it got a little boring. After I tried on a leather skirt, flowered dress, and five different pairs of boots, Mia looked at me.

"Want to play with the dogs?" she asked.

"Yes!" I answered gratefully.

The dogs were completely adorable. Mia said they were Maltese dogs. They could both roll over and sit. Then Mia did this trick where she sneezed and the one called Tiki ran to the tissue box and took a tissue out of it.

"That is truly amazing," I said.

Before I knew it, Mom came to pick me up. On the drive home, she asked me the usual questions about how things went. Then she sneezed.

"That's odd," she said. "My allergies usually don't bug me this time of year."

I knew the dog hair on my clothes was probably making her sneeze, but I didn't say anything.

I wanted to be sure I could go back to Mia's.

CHAPTER 10

The Best Club Ever

The next night I made a batch of cupcakes for Cupcake Friday. I remembered that I hadn't made chocolate cupcakes in a while. They're one of my favorites, and I don't even need Mom to help me make them.

I thought I knew the recipe by heart, but while I was adding the ingredients to the big mixing bowl, I realized that I didn't know how much baking powder to add. So I took the big binder of cupcake recipes from the kitchen shelf and looked up the chocolate cupcakes.

Recipes amaze me. If you follow the directions exactly, you can make something completely awesome.

There should be a recipe for middle school, I thought.

Follow the steps, one by one, and you'd have a perfect middle school experience.

So far, my middle school experience had been kind of a mess. If I had been following a recipe, it probably would look something like this:

Mix together:
1 evil locker
1 confusing best friend
3 mean girls
1 strict math teacher
2 silly arms
Bake until it hardens. If you overbake, go directly to detention.

Luckily, the recipe for the chocolate cupcakes is much better. Soon the whole house smelled like chocolate. After the cupcakes baked and cooled, I spread chocolate icing on them. Then I used a white icing tube to write a name on each cupcake: Katie, Mia, Emma, and Alexis.

Mom came into the kitchen as I was icing.

"Are these the girls you eat lunch with?" she asked.

I nodded.

"You forgot one," Mom said.

I counted again. "No," I said, and then I realized where she was headed.

I froze. Was she going to start asking me about Callie again?

Mom picked up the icing tube and started writing on one of the cupcakes: M-O-M. I relaxed.

"This is going in my lunch bag tomorrow," she said. "Hey, would it be okay if I decorated some for everyone who works in the office?"

"Sure," I said. "I'll help. We can both do Cupcake Fridays."

That's one of the best things about cupcakes. When you make them, there's always a lot to share.

At lunch the next day, I hadn't even sat down yet when everyone started asking about cupcakes.

"So, did you bring them?" Mia asked.

"What kind are they?" asked Alexis.

"I bet they're delicious," added Emma.

"I went for the classic chocolate today," I announced. I opened the lid, and everyone started to ooh and aah.

"We should save them for after lunch," Alexis said.

"Are you kidding? I can't wait!" Mia took hers out of the box.

"I'll wait," Emma said. "I like to save the best

for last—especially in this case. They smell delicious though."

Mia bit into her cupcake. A slow smile came across her face. "You don't know what you're missing."

Alexis and Emma headed to the lunch line. When they got back, Alexis looked agitated.

"You will not believe what those so-called popular girls just did!" she said, fuming. "Emma and I were waiting in line, and Marcus Ridgely was standing in front of us, and that girl Sydney came up with those other girls, and Sydney was like, 'Hey, Marcus, we're behind you, okay?' and then they cut right in front of us!"

"Right in front of us," Emma echoed.

"Did you say anything?" Mia asked.

"Well, no," Alexis admitted. "But what's the point? It's not like they were going to move. They think because they're in some club, that gives them special privileges or something. It's annoying. I can't stand them!"

I looked down at my sandwich. I totally understood why Alexis was upset. But still—she was talking about Callie.

"Alexis, Katie's friend is one of them," Emma said quietly.

Alexis's face turned red. "I know. I'm sorry. I mean, I'm sure your friend is nice. Maybe you get brainwashed or something when you join the Popular Girls Club."

"Not all clubs are bad," Mia said. "At my old school we had a Fashion Club. And a club for kids who like movies. Stuff like that."

"Well, that makes sense," Alexis said. "Those clubs are about something *real*. Not something made-up, like being popular."

I picked up my cupcake. "You know what would be the coolest club ever? A Cupcake Club!" I was mostly kidding around. "You don't have to be popular to join. You just have to like cupcakes."

Alexis grinned. "Now *that* is a club I could like!"

"The Cupcake Club," Emma repeated. "It sounds like fun."

"We should totally do it," Mia said.

"Really?" I asked.

She nodded. "Why not? This school needs more clubs."

I was getting into the idea. "We could have our meetings every Friday at lunch. That's when I bring cupcakes in anyway."

"I like to make cupcakes too," said Emma. "I could bring them in sometimes."

"Maybe we should take turns," Alexis suggested. "I could make up a schedule for all of us."

"Good idea, except I've never made a cupcake before in my life," Mia told us.

"Not even from a mix?" I asked.

Mia shook her head. "We always got them from the bakery down the street. They were soooo good."

"But ours will be better," Alexis said confidently. "Although I don't have a lot of cupcake-making experience either. I know mine won't be as good as yours, Katie."

"It's easy," I assured her. "You just have to follow a recipe."

Then I thought about the first few times I made cupcakes by myself. Mom was always there to help me. She taught me some tricks that weren't in any recipe. "You guys should come to my house this weekend," I blurted out. "We can have a cupcake-making session."

"A cupcake lesson," said Mia. "That sounds like fun."

"I just need to ask my mom," I said. "I'll call everyone tonight, okay?"

I was really excited about the Cupcake Club. Still, I found myself looking over at Callie. Callie loved to make cupcakes as much as I did. It was weird to think of being in a Cupcake Club without Callie.

Would Callie leave the Popular Girls Club to become a member of the Cupcake Club?

Somehow, I didn't think so.

CHAPTER 11

It's Time to Make Some Cupcakes!

So, how many girls are in the club?" my mom asked me as we ate our pizza that night.

"Four," I said. "Me, Mia, Emma, and Alexis."

Mom nodded. "Did you invite Callie to join?"

"I was thinking about it," I said honestly. "I just don't . . . I don't know if she wants to. She kind of made other friends this year."

There, I said it. It was the first time I'd told my mom about what happened with Callie. I felt relieved.

"That happens sometimes," Mom said gently. "People grow up, and they change sometimes. It happened to me in fifth grade. A new girl came to our school, and my best friend, Sally, suddenly became best friends with the new girl instead. I was really, really sad. But then I met new friends."

It was hard to imagine my mom as a little girl. I pictured her going to school in her dentist coat. But I knew what she meant.

"Callie and I said we'd still hang out sometimes," I told my mom. "I think I'm going to text her."

I sent the text after dinner.

> Hey Cal. Making cupcakes tomorrow at 2. Wanna come?

Callie texted me back.

> Sounds like fun! Wish I could go but I'm going to the mall. Maybe next time?

I texted back.

> Sure.

I was a little disappointed, but not too much. I knew tomorrow was going to be fun, even without Callie.

"Callie's not coming," I told my mom. "Can we call the other girls now?"

"Of course," Mom replied. "I was thinking we could do simple cupcakes—vanilla with chocolate icing. I think we're out of sugar, but we can shop in the morning."

"Let's do something different on top," I suggested. "What about those little chocolate candies covered with white candy dots? That would be cool with a vanilla and chocolate cupcake."

Mom grinned. "Perfect!"

"And, um, Mom?" I said. "We might, you know, need some help, but I'm thinking that if we're going to be a Cupcake Club, we should learn to make them on our own."

"Oh!" Mom said, and I was afraid I hurt her feelings. "Well, I'll have to be home, of course, but that sounds right to me. You can just yell if you need me."

Sometimes Mom surprises me. For someone so corny, she can sometimes be very cool.

By two o'clock the next day, we were ready for the first official meeting of the Cupcake Club to begin. I helped Mom wash the yellow tiles on the floor and scrub the kitchen table until there wasn't a crumb on it. We got out our cupcake tins, the flour sifter, Mom's big red mixer, the glass measuring cup, and the little cup with the bird on it that holds the measuring spoons.

Finally, the doorbell rang. Mia was standing there.

"Hi," she said when I opened the door.

Then a blue minivan pulled up in front of the house, and Emma and Alexis got out, along with the woman driving the van. She was short, with blond hair that she wore in a ponytail. She was wearing a sweatshirt with a hummingbird on it, jeans, and sneakers.

"You must be Katie," she said, holding out her hand to shake mine. "I'm Wendy Taylor, Emma's mom. I was hoping I could meet your mom."

My mom magically appeared in the doorway. "Wendy, nice to meet you in person. I'm Sharon. Please come inside."

The moms walked in ahead of us, and Emma gave me an apologetic look.

"Sorry," she whispered. "My mom is really over-protective."

I smiled. "I know how you feel. My mom's the same way."

I led the girls into the kitchen.

"Whoa. It's like cupcake central," Mia remarked.

"We bake a lot of cupcakes," I admitted. "So we've got all the stuff."

We have a big closet in our kitchen that Mom calls the pantry. One whole shelf has all the stuff we need to bake cupcakes, cakes, and cookies: icing tubes, sprinkles, plastic decorations like balloons and flowers that you can stick into the top of a cupcake—stuff like that.

I opened the door to show the girls. "Everything we need is in here," I said. I started grabbing things and handing them to everyone. "Flour. Baking powder. Sugar. Vanilla."

"Don't you use a mix?" Alexis asked.

"Mom says it's just as easy to do it from scratch, and at least you know what's going in it," I said.

I got two eggs out of the refrigerator and picked up the butter that had been softening on the counter.

"That should do it for now." I nodded to the sink. "Before we start, we should all wash our hands."

"Wow, you are a strict teacher," Mia joked.

I laughed. "Can you imagine if Mrs. Moore taught us how to make cupcakes?" I did my best to imitate her voice, which was kind of deep and a little bit musical. "Concentration is the key to succeeding in this class, students! Without concentration, you won't be able to make your cupcakes."

Alexis and Emma started giggling like crazy.

"That is too perfect," Alexis said. "Can you do Ms. Biddle?"

I thought for a minute. Ms. Biddle had an upbeat

voice, like a cheerleader. And she always made everything about science.

"Who wants to make a hypothesis about how these cupcakes will taste?" I asked.

Mia raised her hand. "Delicious!"

"Wait, I can do Ms. Chen," Alexis said. She made her back really straight. "Look alive, people! It's time to make some cupcakes!"

By then I was cracking up so hard, my stomach hurt. That's when Mom walked in.

"I never knew cupcakes were so funny," she said.

I went back into my Mrs. Moore voice. "You are late, Mrs. Brown! Detention!"

That just made everyone laugh even harder. Mom shook her head and smiled.

"Emma, your mom will be back for you and Alexis at four," she told us. "So, girls, get started. I'll be in the den if you need me."

I kind of led the cupcake demonstration. First we mixed the eggs, butter, and sugar together in the mixer. We added the vanilla. Then we sifted the dry ingredients together in another bowl: the flour, baking powder, and salt. Everybody took turns measuring. When it was Alexis's turn to sift the flour, it puffed up like a cloud and settled on her face like powder.

"No flour in this classroom! Detention!" I cried out in my Mrs. Moore voice, and we all laughed again.

Then we slowly mixed the dry ingredients and wet ingredients together using the mixer. When it was all done, Mom popped in to check on us and showed us how to use an ice-cream scoop to put the perfect amount of batter into each cupcake cup, which is good because I always forget that part and they kind of get big and explode. Then we had to wait while the cupcakes baked. That was okay, because we had to clean up the whole mess we made. When the cupcakes were cooling, we used the mixer again to make chocolate icing.

I've always thought that icing the cupcakes is the hardest part. Mom got us special flat knives to use, but it's still kind of hard.

Alexis and Emma were struggling with the icing, just like me. But when Mia put it on, it was smooth and perfect.

"I thought you never did this before?" I asked.

"I haven't," Mia said. She looked really happy. "I guess I have a hidden talent for icing cupcakes."

"Mine looks like a very sad cupcake," Emma said, holding hers up.

"I know what will make it happy," I told her. I

took out the bag of chocolate candies Mom and I had bought and put one right in the middle. "See? Perfect!"

"It does look better," Emma agreed.

Everyone dug into the bag and we decorated the top of each cupcake. Emma, Alexis, and I put a single candy in the middle of each one. Mia got really creative. On one, she put the candies all around the edge of the cupcake. It looked really cool. She also made some look like flowers.

"You're a natural," I told her.

Mia beamed. "Can I try making the cupcakes for lunch next Friday? I really think I can do it."

"Sure," I said. "You can always call if you need help."

Before we knew it, it was four o'clock. Mom had small boxes for everyone so they could take some cupcakes home. Emma took home the most: one for each of her parents and her brothers.

There was some stuff to clean up after the girls left, but I didn't mind. Mom helped.

"It looks like the Cupcake Club got off to a good start," she remarked.

I smiled at her. "I think you're right!"

CHAPTER 12

Middle School Roller Coaster

Something happened after we formed the Cupcake Club: Middle school got a little bit easier.

Honest! For example, my locker started opening up on the first try. Coincidence? I don't think so. Alexis says I probably just loosened up the insides of the lock so it opens more easily, but I don't believe it. I'd rather think that the superpowers of the Cupcake Club defeated my evil alien locker.

Now, take math class. I wish I could say that Mrs. Moore was suddenly nicer, but I can't. What happens now is that every time Mrs. Moore says something serious, or threatens to give us all detention, I write down what she says so I can use it the next time I do an impression of her. She's not so scary anymore.

Not that everything is perfect. Take gym class. On Tuesday we were picking teams for flag football, and Sydney said, "Don't pick Katie unless you want to lose!" She said it really loudly, and a bunch of kids laughed. Sometimes I feel like saying something, but I don't. I keep waiting for the time when we have races outside on the track. I've been a faster runner than Sydney ever since third grade.

Then something happened in English class on Wednesday. It didn't happen to me, exactly, but to another member of the Cupcake Club: Alexis.

Here's what happened. At the beginning of class Mrs. Castillo told us she was giving us a vocabulary worksheet for homework. But she didn't hand it out. Then, right before the bell rang, Alexis raised her hand.

"Mrs. Castillo, what about the vocab worksheet?" she asked.

Everyone groaned. Everyone except for me, Mia, and Emma.

We know that Alexis is just like that. She likes to do things exactly the way you're supposed to. She especially likes to make teachers happy.

As you can guess, nobody was happy with Alexis.

"Thanks a lot, Alexis," Eddie Rossi said from the back of the room.

"Yeah, what, are you in love with homework?" added Devin Jaworski.

"Please settle down," ordered Mrs. Castillo. "You're lucky Alexis reminded me. Otherwise you'd have double homework tomorrow night."

But of course that didn't make anyone feel better. When the bell rang and we poured into the hallway, a lot of the boys were still giving Alexis a hard time.

"Teacher's pet!"

"Thanks for the homework!"

Alexis started to look like she might cry. I felt bad for her.

"Leave her alone," Mia said bravely, and we all hurried off to our lockers.

That was pretty much the worst thing that happened all week—until Cupcake Friday.

Mia came into the cafeteria carrying a really pretty pink bakery box. She opened the lid to reveal four perfect cupcakes with chocolate icing dotted with chocolate candies.

"They're so pretty," Emma said.

"I hope they taste good," Mia said with a small frown. "We didn't have any vanilla. And I lost count when I was putting in the teaspoons of salt. I might have put in an extra amount."

Alexis pounded her fist on the table. "Let the second meeting of the Cupcake Club begin!"

That's when Sydney and Brenda—I mean, Bella—walked by. Sydney stopped cold.

"Cupcake Club?" she asked. "Are you serious? What is this, third grade?"

"Yeah, that's so lame!" Bella added, making a big deal out of rolling her eyes.

"Not as lame as a Popular Girls Club," Alexis said under her breath.

Sydney raised an eyebrow. "Excuse me? Did you say something?"

Alexis, Emma, and I were all kind of afraid of Sydney. But not Mia.

"Maybe I'll bring some next time for you to try," she said coolly.

Sydney snorted. "No thanks," she said, and then she and Bella walked away.

"Well, that was fun," I said.

"Who wants a cupcake?" Mia asked.

We all reached for one, but I had a little knot in my stomach. I watched Bella and Sydney slide into their table with Callie. They were all reading some magazine. I tried not to look.

The cupcakes were good. They tasted a tiny bit weird because of the extra salt, but not too weird.

Plus the icing was especially delicious.

"Nice job," I told Mia, and she smiled at me. I could tell she was proud.

That same day, when the eighth-period bell rang, I was walking to my locker and I saw Mia talking to a bunch of girls from her class. They were all laughing.

For a second I got a strange feeling. Then it hit me. Not that I care about how "cool" people are or anything, but Mia is a lot cooler than me. What if she got bored with the Cupcake Club? What if she found other friends, like Callie had?

"There's no use in worrying about what might happen," Mom always says. "Concentrate on how things are right now."

I remember a lot of stuff Mom tells me, usually because she says it over and over again. Also, it's just me and her most of the time, so I guess she's a pretty big part of my life.

Anyway, I'm glad I remembered that. Because right now, Mia was my friend. She rode the bus with me every day and ate lunch with me every day. She invited me to her house and baked cupcakes for the Cupcake Club.

Maybe in the future that would change, just like things had changed with Callie over the summer.

But for now, everything with Mia was all right.

Mia saw me standing there and waved.

"Hey, Katie! See you on the bus!"

See? Sometimes Mom is right.

CHAPTER 13

Alexis Has an Idea

𝒜 did see Callie a few times over the next few weeks. One night my mom invited the Wilsons over for Italian food night. It's kind of a tradition between our families, like the Labor Day barbecue. My mom makes tons of pasta and salad. She lights candles on our dining-room table, puts out a red-and-white-checkered tablecloth, and goes all out, of course. But it's actually usually a pretty fun night.

Then another night Callie called and invited me to come over and watch the first episode of *Singing Stars* on TV. It's our favorite show. I had a good time, even though Callie kept getting texts on her cell phone the whole time.

Mostly I hung out with the Cupcake Club. Everyone came over one Saturday, and Mom showed us how she makes her P-B-and-J cupcakes. And one night Mia invited me over for dinner. Her mom got takeout food from an Indian restaurant. I'd never eaten Indian food before, and it was good—and spicy. Mia's mom and stepdad were nice, and her stepbrother, Dan, seemed nice too. Which was kind of a surprise, because Mia is always saying what a beast he is.

Oh, and I got detention from Mrs. Moore. Twice. But the whole class had it, so it wasn't so bad.

And the best thing was that I could talk to Mia, Emma, and Alexis about it. That's mostly what the Cupcake Club did. We baked cupcakes; we ate cupcakes; and we talked about stuff.

Things were not perfect, but they were good.

One Monday we were eating lunch, and everyone was talking about the announcement that Principal LaCosta had made that morning after the Pledge of Allegiance.

"This morning your homeroom teacher will be distributing permission slips for the first dance of the year," she said. "Please hand them in by next Monday if you're going to attend. This year's dance will be bigger than ever. That afternoon, we'll be holding a special fund-raising event for the school. Check your flyer for details."

Now we were sitting around the lunch table, looking at the flyers.

"I always heard we had dances in middle school," Alexis said. "I just didn't think it would be so soon."

"Do you think we actually have to *dance* at the dance?" I asked. My mom loves the movie *Grease*, and in that movie the high school kids twirl and throw one another in the air and stuff like that. I didn't think I could do that in a million years.

"We had dances at my old school," Mia informed us. "Sometimes people danced. Mostly everyone just hung around and talked."

"Did boys and girls dance together?" Emma asked. She sounded a little worried.

"Sometimes," Mia replied.

We were quiet for a minute. I think all of us except for Mia were feeling nervous about the dance.

"Did you see the part about the fund-raiser?" I asked. "It's going to be in the parking lot of the school. If you have an idea to make money for the school, you can set up a booth. The booth that makes the most money will get a prize."

"I heard the basketball team is doing a dunking booth with all of the gym teachers," Alexis reported. "I bet that will make a lot of money."

"Maybe we could have a dunking booth for math teachers," I joked.

Over at the PGC table, Sydney was talking in a loud voice on purpose.

"Our club is going to have the best booth at the fund-raiser," Sydney bragged. "That's why we have to keep it top secret."

Alexis rolled her eyes. "This is supposed to be for the whole school, not just the Popular Girls Club," she said. "Only Sydney can turn a good cause into something about herself."

"I wonder what their top secret idea is?" Emma asked.

Alexis had that look on her face where you know the wheels of her brain are spinning faster than a car's.

"You know, I bet we can raise a lot of money just by selling cupcakes," she said. "Who could say no to a cupcake for a good cause?"

"That's not a bad idea," Mia agreed. "But we'd have to make a lot of cupcakes, wouldn't we?"

Alexis took out her notebook and started scribbling numbers.

"There are about four hundred kids in the school," she said. "Let's say half of them go to the dance. That's two hundred. Then there are teachers. And parents, and younger brothers and sisters. So let's say that's another two hundred people, for a total of four hundred. Now let's say that half of those people buy cupcakes—"

"We'd need two hundred cupcakes," I said, and then gasped. "Oh no! I did math. Mrs. Moore must be getting through to me."

"That sounds like a lot of cupcakes," Emma said.

"Not really," Alexis said. "It's about seventeen dozen. We could bake a few dozen at a time over four or five days. Since it's for the school, I bet we can ask our parents to donate the ingredients. If we sell each cupcake for fifty cents, we'd make a hundred dollars."

"Fifty cents?" Mia asked. "At the cupcake shop in Manhattan, they charge five dollars a cupcake. Katie's cupcakes are just as good as theirs."

Alexis's eyes were wide. "Who would pay five dollars for one cupcake?"

"Maybe we could charge two dollars a cupcake," Emma suggested.

"That could work," I chimed in. "If we sold all of the cupcakes, we'd make four hundred dollars. We might even win the contest."

"We should definitely do this," Mia said, her eyes shining with excitement.

"I'm sure this is better than whatever Sydney is planning," Alexis said smugly.

I looked over at the PGC table. I wasn't really thinking about beating Sydney. I was thinking about Callie. She wasn't too interested in the Cupcake Club when I talked about it. But if we won the fund-raising contest . . . maybe Callie would be convinced she was in the wrong club.

"I'm in," I said. "So how exactly are we going to make two hundred cupcakes?"

CHAPTER 14

The Mixed-up Cupcakes

"We should have a meeting so we can figure this out," Alexis suggested. "We could do it at my house this time. How about Saturday?"

"I'm going to my dad's this weekend," Mia said.

"Next weekend should be fine," Emma said. "It's a month until the dance, anyway."

"We need to figure out what kind of cupcake to make," I reminded everyone.

"We can do that next week," Alexis said. "We'll work out a schedule, too."

So the following Saturday I showed up at Alexis's front door with a whole bunch of recipes and enough ingredients for a couple dozen. If we were going to decide on a cupcake, we would have to do some research.

Alexis lives in a brick house with a very neat front lawn. The bushes on either side of the white front steps are the kind that are trimmed into a perfect globe shape.

Alexis looked surprised when she answered the door.

"Hi, Katie," she said. "What's all that?"

"It's for our meeting," I explained. "So we can experiment with cupcake flavors."

"Oh," she said. "I thought we were just going to talk about it."

"Why just talk when we can taste?" I asked.

Alexis led me into the kitchen. I've been in her house a few times so far, and I'm always amazed how clean it is in there. For example, there is nothing on the kitchen counter, not even a toaster. Our counter has a toaster, the big red mixer, a cookie jar shaped like an apple, Mom's spice rack, and usually a bowl of fruit.

Alexis's mom was at the kitchen table, setting up a pitcher of water and glasses for our meeting, along with a bowl of grapes. I noticed there was a piece of paper and pencil at each of the four places around the table.

Mrs. Becker was wearing a button-down light blue shirt and dark blue dress pants. I've never seen her wear jeans, not even on a Saturday. Her hair is auburn like Alexis's, but it's cut short.

"Hello, Katie," she said when she saw me. She noticed the bag I was carrying. "Did you bring snacks? How nice."

"It's actually supplies, so we can make test cupcakes," I told her.

"You mean you'll be baking?" she asked. "Oh dear. I didn't know you'd be baking today, Alexis."

"We'll clean up when we're done, Mom," Alexis said. "Promise."

"It's true. We clean up all the time when we bake at my house," I added.

Mrs. Becker gave a little sigh. "All right. But let me know when you are ready to turn on the oven!"

She hurried out of the kitchen.

"Mom doesn't like it when the plan changes," Alexis explained. "Especially when there's a mess involved."

"I promise we won't make a mess," I said. Then I remembered what my kitchen usually looks like when I bake cupcakes. "Well, not too much of a mess, anyway."

Emma and Mia arrived next, at the same time. Alexis neatly piled up the pencils and paper, and

I took all of the ingredients I'd brought out of my bag. Besides the basic cupcake-making stuff, I had mini marshmallows, chocolate chips, nuts, sprinkles, red-hot candies, tubes of icing and food coloring, and a jar of cherries—just about everything I could grab from the pantry.

"Mmm, everything looks so yummy," Mia said.

"Well, I was thinking that we have to make a really *incredible* cupcake if we're going to sell a lot," I said. "Something we've never done before."

"How do we do that?" Emma asked.

"We experiment," I said. "Mom and I do it all the time. That's how we came up with our famous banana split cupcake. Only I didn't have any bananas, so we'll have to come up with something else."

I turned to Alexis. "Do you have a mixer?" I asked.

"Not the kind you have," she replied. "It's the one you hold in your hand."

"That's fine," I said. "First we need to make a regular vanilla batter."

I had made so many vanilla cupcakes over the last few weeks that I didn't need a recipe at all. Pretty soon we had a perfect bowl of batter ready.

"Now we just have to figure out what to add in," I said.

"Everyone loves chocolate chips," Mia suggested. We stirred some in.

"Marshmallows go well with chocolate," said Alexis.

Emma nodded. "Definitely."

We added some mini marshmallows to the batter.

"What about nuts?" Emma asked. "It might be good to have something crunchy in there."

"Some people are allergic to nuts," Alexis pointed out.

"That's true," I said. "But sprinkles are crunchy too. Maybe we could put sprinkles in."

Alexis wrinkled her nose. "You mean put them *in* a cupcake instead of on top?"

"Why not?" I asked.

Nobody had a good argument. I dumped in half a bottle of rainbow sprinkles.

"They look good," Mia said. "And I don't think there's room in the bowl for anything else."

We scooped all of the batter into the cupcake tins Alexis put out for us. Because of all the stuff we mixed in, there was a lot of batter left over.

"I don't have any more pans," Alexis said.

"No problem," I told her. "We can always bake more when the first batch cools."

Mrs. Becker came in to preheat the oven for us.

She raised her eyebrow when she saw our cupcakes.

"My, those look interesting," she said.

"Wait till you taste it, Mom," Alexis told her. "You're going to love it!"

While the cupcakes baked, we whipped up some plain vanilla icing.

"Should we add anything into the icing?" I asked.

"I think the cupcakes have enough inside them," Mia said.

"Good point," I said.

We cleaned up our mess while we waited for the cupcakes to bake. When the timer rang, Mrs. Becker helped us with the oven.

"Do you take them out now?" she asked.

"We need to test them first," I said.

Mom had taught me how to stick a toothpick into the middle of a cupcake. If it came out clean, it was done. But if it had batter on it, the cupcake needed to cook more.

I stuck a toothpick into the middle of one of our mixed-up cupcakes. When I took it out, it wasn't clean. But it didn't have batter on it. It had gooey marshmallow, chocolate, and a sprinkle stuck to it.

I frowned. "I'm not sure if it's done or not," I said.

Alexis looked over my shoulder. "They look

done. They're a little brown on top, see?"

I realized there would be no sure way to tell if the cupcakes were done. We might as well take them out. Besides, I was dying to try one! The delicious smell of baking cupcakes was taking over my brain.

We put the cupcakes on a rack to cool. Normally, we talk a lot when we're waiting for cupcakes to cool off. But that day we stared at our cupcakes, like we were going to cool them off with the amazing power of our minds alone.

Finally Mia blurted out, "Maybe we should try them without icing. You know, to get a true sense of how they taste."

"That sounds very logical to me," I said.

We each picked up a cupcake. They were warm, but cool enough to handle. I unwrapped the paper and took a bite. A hot, gooey mess of chocolate and marshmallow exploded in my mouth.

"Mmmmmm," was all I could say.

Alexis had a weird look on her face. "It's too sweet!"

"There's no such thing as too sweet," I told her, and Emma nodded in agreement.

Mia had another complaint. "They're kind of messy," she said, wiping her hand on a napkin.

"Let's see what my mom thinks," Alexis said.

She left the kitchen and returned with both parents. Mr. Becker was tall and skinny with curly hair and glasses like his wife.

"I think you girls have a great fund-raising idea," he said. "Everybody loves cupcakes!"

Alexis handed one to each parent. "They're not iced yet," she said. "They might taste different when they're iced."

We held our breath as Mr. and Mrs. Becker bit into their cupcakes. Mrs. Becker made the same weird face that Alexis had.

"My, they're very sweet!" she said.

"They're tasty," said Mr. Becker. "But I'll tell you something. I'm not a big fan of marshmallows. Never liked them. You know what makes me happy? A plain vanilla cupcake. Mmm."

I thought of Callie's dad. "I think that's a parent thing. Parents like vanilla cupcakes."

"And don't forget, parents are a big part of our sales," Alexis reminded us.

I was starting to feel discouraged. "But plain vanilla cupcakes are boring! We need our cupcakes to be extra special so everyone wants them."

"Well, maybe they could *look* special," Mia said.

"What do you mean?" I asked.

"Well, this is a school fund-raiser, right? Maybe

they could be in the school colors or something," she said.

I immediately knew what she was talking about. "Mrs. Becker, can we have another bowl, please?"

I scooped half of the vanilla frosting we had made into the new bowl. Then I put a few drops of blue food coloring into one bowl, and a few drops of yellow into the other. Emma helped me stir them up.

"Make that one bluer," Mia said, pointing.

After a couple of more drops, we had the perfect blue and yellow—the official colors of Park Street Middle School.

"Mia, do your magic," I told her.

Mia expertly iced one cupcake with blue frosting and another cupcake with yellow frosting. Then she used an icing tube to write "PS" in yellow on the blue cupcake, and "PS" in blue on the yellow cupcake.

"Just imagine there are plain vanilla cupcakes inside," Mia said, holding them out to us.

"They're just right!" said Mrs. Becker.

"I bet you'll sell a hundred of those," agreed Mr. Becker.

"*Two* hundred," Alexis cheered.

"We will," I said confidently. "We are definitely

going to win this contest. We just have to do one thing."

"What?" Alexis asked.

"We have to *bake* two hundred cupcakes!"

CHAPTER 15

How to Bake
Two Hundred Cupcakes

Even though I was disappointed that we were making plain vanilla cupcakes, I loved Mia's cupcake design. And the next Cupcake Friday, Emma brought in cupcakes for us that she made herself.

When I bit into one, I tasted chocolate chips and sprinkles!

"I left out the marshmallows, so they wouldn't be too sweet or too sticky," she said. "What do you think?"

"I think they're amazing," I said.

Emma blushed a little. "Well, I really did like our mixed-up cupcakes."

That made me feel better. At least Emma liked them!

As we ate our cupcakes, we went over our plan

for the next week. Our parents had agreed to let us bake cupcakes once a day for four days before the contest. We would start baking on Tuesday and finish baking on Friday night. Then Saturday morning, we would ice and decorate every single one. We had to promise to get all of our homework done right after school.

Mom said we could do all the baking at our house. Each one of us would take turns bringing the ingredients and cupcake liners.

Alexis had the whole thing mapped out on a chart.

"Tuesday night, Katie will provide the supplies," she said, reading out loud. "I'll bring them Wednesday, Emma can bring them Thursday, and Mia will do Friday. Then Saturday, we'll all chip in for the icing. We'll have to make four dozen cupcakes every night, and do an extra dozen on Friday. Then we'll have four left over."

I leaned across the table to get a better look at the chart. Alexis had worked out a whole system with stickers. One cupcake-shaped sticker equaled a dozen cupcakes. It all looked very complicated.

"It looks a lot harder to bake two hundred cupcakes than I thought," I said.

I heard a laugh. When I turned around, I saw

Sydney and Maggie standing by the table.

"I saw the sign-up sheets for the fund-raiser," Sydney said. "You're doing a bake sale? Now *that's* really original."

"Bake sales are so boring!" Maggie added.

You know what's boring and unoriginal? I thought. *Following Sydney around and repeating everything she says like a parrot.*

I thought it, but I wasn't brave enough to say it. As usual, though, Mia wasn't afraid to speak up at all.

"Everybody likes cupcakes," Mia said. "So, what are you guys doing? On the fund-raising sheet it just says 'Popular Girls Club.'"

"It's top secret," Sydney said. "Nobody has ever done what we're planning. We're going to blow everyone away."

"Not everyone," said Alexis under her breath.

But Sydney and Maggie didn't hear her and walked away.

"I wonder what they're planning?" Emma asked worriedly. "I bet it's really good."

"I bet they haven't even thought of it yet," I said. "Otherwise, they wouldn't be bragging about their idea to everyone."

Alexis laughed. "You're probably right."

111

After Sydney's comments, I wanted to win that contest more than ever. We had a recipe. We had a plan.

Now we just had to make it happen.

Our first baking night was the Tuesday night before the fund-raiser. I could tell Mom was really excited too. She even bought extra cupcake pans for us to use.

Mia, Alexis, and Emma all got to my house right at seven o'clock. Mom gave us a little pep talk—and some instructions.

"There are enough pans here for four dozen cupcakes," she said. "But I wouldn't make a double batch of batter. Baking is tricky. Make one batch first, put it in the oven, and then start the second batch. Then you'll end up with perfect cupcakes."

"Thanks, Mrs. Brown," Mia said.

"Now, how about a huddle?" Mom asked.

Oh, Mom. . . . To make her happy, we all put our hands on top of one another's. Mom led the cheer.

"Goooooooo Cupcake Club!"

Then we got to work. By then, we were getting into a cupcake groove. Emma liked sifting the flour, Alexis liked measuring things, Mia liked mixing things, and I liked cracking the eggs. We had the first batch of two dozen cupcakes done in record time, and then the phone rang.

I wiped off my hands and picked it up. "Hey, Katie." It was Callie. "I tried texting you. Are you watching *Singing Stars*? Ryan just advanced to the finals. Can you believe it?"

I realized that I totally forgot it was time for *Singing Stars*. "Uh, I'm not watching it," I said. "We're making cupcakes for the fund-raiser."

"Hey, Katie, how many eggs is it again?" Mia called out.

"Oh," Callie said. "You have company. Sorry to bother you." There was a little silence. "Well, I'll talk to you tomorrow."

"Text me with the results, okay?" I asked.

"Sure," she said, and then she hung up.

I felt a little sad for a minute. Callie belonged in the Cupcake Club. She could be having so much fun with us if she wanted to.

"Earth to Katie. How many eggs?" Mia asked.

"Oh, sorry. Two," I replied.

By the time Alexis's dad came by to pick up everyone, we had four dozen cupcakes in boxes stored safely in our freezer.

"Forty-eight down, one hundred and fifty-two to go," Mia said as they were leaving.

"Actually, it's one hundred and fifty-six, since we're making two hundred and four cupcakes," Alexis pointed out.

"One hundred and fifty-six?" I cried. We had worked really hard tonight. Yet it didn't seem like we'd done much, after all.

After my friends left I flopped on the couch—for about five seconds.

"Time to jump in the shower, Katie," Mom told me. "I don't want you getting to bed late."

I rolled over onto the floor. "You'll have to drag me."

"Hmm," Mom said. "Maybe all this cupcake baking is too much for you."

I jumped to my feet. Mom always knows how to get me.

"Nope. I'm fine!" I told her. Then I ran to the bathroom.

As I drifted off to sleep that night, I thought about what the instructions would look like for someone making two hundred cupcakes.

How to Make 200 Cupcakes:
1. Do homework in a dentist office.
2. Eat dinner.
3. Clean up after dinner.

4. Make four dozen cupcakes.

5. Clean up after making four dozen cupcakes.

6. Shower.

7. Rinse.

8. Sleep.

9. Repeat.

10. Repeat.

11. Repeat.

CHAPTER 16

The Purple Dress

*T*wo hundred one, two hundred two, two hundred three, two hundred four!"

We counted together as the last cupcake—the last of seventeen dozen exactly—went into its box.

"We did it! Woo-hoo!" I cheered. Everyone kind of jumped around.

"You know, it's funny that there are exactly four cupcakes left over," Alexis pointed out. "One for each of us."

"I think that's a sign," Mia said. "We need to eat those four to make it an even two hundred."

"But four cupcakes equals eight dollars," Alexis reminded us.

"I know," I chimed in. "But maybe it's, like, a good luck thing."

That satisfied Alexis. "Good point. We should probably taste them anyway, to make sure they're okay."

The vanilla cupcakes were delicious, even without the icing.

"So we'll meet here tomorrow at eight to ice them," I reminded everyone. "The fund-raiser starts at noon."

The doorbell rang, and Alexis's mom came to pick up her and Emma. Then Mia's stepbrother beeped his horn outside.

"Mom and I will pick you up after dinner," Mia told me.

"Okay. I'll be ready," I said.

I forgot to mention that on Friday we baked the cupcakes right after school because we didn't have to do our homework right away. The night before, Mia had had an idea about how we should spend Friday night.

"What is everybody wearing to the dance?" she wanted to know.

Alexis shrugged. "I don't know. What I always wear."

"I was thinking about wearing my favorite dress," Emma said. "The one with the pink flowers."

"I didn't even think about it," I admitted. "Do

we have to get dressed up to go to the dance?"

"Well, no," Mia admitted. "You don't *have* to. But it's fun. I was thinking that tomorrow night we should all go to the mall and look for dresses to wear."

"I can't," Alexis said. "We're going to my aunt's for dinner."

"I'll probably just wear the dress I have," Emma said.

Mia looked at me. "Come on, Katie. What do you say?"

"I have to ask my mom," I said. Honestly, I don't like shopping at all. But I think Mia could make anything fun. "But yeah, why not?"

My mom agreed (after talking to Mia's mom, of course), and so Ms. Vélaz and Mia picked me up at seven.

The Westgrove Mall is really big, with a lot of buildings all connected together. It reminds me of a big maze. When we walked through the doors, Ms. Vélaz turned to us.

"What store are we going to first?" she asked.

Mia looked horrified. "Mom, seriously?"

"Of course! This is a big mall," her mom pointed out. "Besides, I promised Mrs. Brown that I'd stick with you girls."

I felt like sinking into the floor. My mom sticks to me like glue when we go to the mall. She used to make me wear one of those kid leashes until I was five. Here I was, in middle school, and I could still feel the invisible leash tugging at me.

Ms. Vélaz must have seen the look on my face. "You know, you girls are lucky to have an expert fashion consultant accompanying you!"

Mia grabbed me by the arm. "Come on. There's a supercute store right around the corner."

Mia's mom walked slowly behind us as we raced into the store. Loud dance music blared through the speakers. The store was pretty crowded with girls looking through racks of dresses, shirts, skirts, and jeans.

Mia skidded to a stop in front of a black dress with a zipper down the front.

"This is so cute," she said. "Katie, you should try it on."

"I don't know," I said. "It's black. Black clothes remind me of vampires."

Mia looked me up and down. I was wearing a pair of old jeans with a rip in the knee and a red T-shirt with a peace sign on it.

"So you like bright colors," she said. "What else do you like?"

I shrugged. "I don't know. I don't know what's in style and what's not. When I go shopping with my mom, we get some jeans and then I pick out whatever shirts I like."

"So you can do that with a dress, too," Mia said. "Just look around and see what you like."

That sounded easy enough. I started looking through the racks of clothes with Mia. At first I was just confused. There were so many dresses! And even though they were different colors and different styles, they kind of all looked the same to me.

Then a splash of purple caught my eye. I walked over to a display with a headless mannequin wearing a purple dress. It was *really* purple. Grape jelly purple. But I liked it. It had short sleeves and a straight skirt with a black belt around the middle.

I took one off the rack. "I kind of like this," I told Mia. "It looks good on the mannequin. But she doesn't have a head, so anything would look good on her, I guess."

"No, I like it!" Mia said. I could tell she was excited. "Try it on!"

The dressing rooms were lined up on the side wall. A salesperson used a key to open up one of the silver doors for me. I stepped inside and tried on the dress.

I looked at myself in the mirror. "Not bad," I had to admit.

Then I heard Mia's voice outside. "Katie, come out! I am dying to see how you look!"

I cautiously stepped outside the dressing room. Mia's eyes got wide when she saw me.

"Ooh, it's perfect! Turn around!" she ordered.

I felt like the world's worst fashion model as I turned in a circle for Mia's inspection.

"You have got to get it," she said. "Wear it with some short black boots and it'll be fabulous."

"What if I don't have short black boots?" I asked.

"Then you can borrow mine!"

I looked at the price tag. It cost less than the money Mom had given me to spend. "I think I'll get it," I said. "That was easy!"

Then I heard a familiar loud voice nearby. "That dress is gross, Mags. I wouldn't wear that to gym class."

Sydney! I had to get inside that dressing room before she saw me. I turned to run, but it was too late.

"Isn't it a little too early for Halloween, Katie?"

There she goes, I thought. If I couldn't escape, I might as well face her.

I spun around. "What do you mean, Sydney?"

"Well, that's a grape costume, isn't it?" she asked. "No, wait—you're that purple dinosaur."

She made me so angry! I wished I had some great comeback to give her. But as usual, she left me tongue-tied.

"You know, Sydney, violet was a hot runway color this fall," Mia said in that supercool tone of hers. "I was just reading about it in the color trends column in *Fashion Weekly*."

Now it was Sydney's turn to get tongue-tied. But she managed to recover. "Violet or not, it's an ugly dress."

For the first time ever, I thought of something to say to Sydney. And I wasn't afraid to say it, either. Maybe Mia was rubbing off on me a little.

"I don't care if *you* think it's ugly," I said. "I like it."

Then I marched back into my dressing room and out of the corner of my eye I saw Mia smirk. My heart was pounding. Something about that dress made me feel good. Good enough to tell stupid old Sydney to shut up.

And that's why my purple dress is still my favorite dress to this day. And as it turns out—it's my lucky one, too.

CHAPTER 17

PGC's Secret Is Revealed!

Saturday morning was, as the skateboarding dudes in my school say, intense. Mom and I got up super-early and started mixing batches and batches of icing. The girls came over, and Emma's mom came over to help too.

It took hours, but we got everything done. My mom and Emma's mom iced the cupcakes with me. Mia wrote the letters on them with her perfect handwriting. Alexis and Emma made a big cardboard sign for the table that said CUPCAKES $2.00. Then they helped us with the icing.

By eleven o'clock we had two hundred perfect cupcakes. We carefully transferred them to Emma's mom's minivan, and she drove them to the school. My mom and I brought the sign, a cash box, one blue and one yellow tablecloth, and plastic trays for the cupcakes.

The day was perfect for a fund-raiser—sunny but not too hot. When we got to the school, the big parking lot was roped off with police tape. There were a bunch of canopies set up in a square all around the lot. Blue and yellow balloons tied to the canopies waved and wiggled in the air. We searched around until we found a table with a note that said CUPCAKE CLUB on it.

We started setting up. We spread out the blue tablecloth and then draped the yellow one over it in another direction so you could see both colors. Alexis and Emma taped up their sign. We put about half the cupcakes on platters. Then we stood back and checked out our table.

"Not bad," I said.

"It's a little flat," Mia said, turning her head sideways. "Maybe next time we could put the platters on pillars or something so that some are high and some are low."

Mom walked up behind us and put her arm around me.

"Well, *I* think it looks perfect!" she said. "Why don't you girls go stand in front of the table? I'll take a picture."

We quickly lined up: me, Mia, Alexis, and then Emma.

"Say 'cupcake'!" Mom called out.

"Cupcake!" we shouted.

Alexis glanced at her watch. "We still have fifteen minutes. Let's check out the competition."

"Good idea," I agreed.

We walked around. There must have been about a dozen tables besides ours. The basketball team was still setting up their dunking booth at the end of the parking lot. The girls' soccer team had a booth where they would take your picture, print it out, and put it in a frame. Then you could decorate the frame with shapes like stars and soccer balls. Then we walked past the Chess Club's table.

"Oh, no!" Emma cried. "A bake sale!"

The table was covered with paper plates topped with cookies, brownies, and yes—cupcakes.

"I think our table stands out more," Mia whispered to us. "And they don't have special Park Street Middle School cupcakes, either."

"Besides, they have mostly cookies," Alexis pointed out. "And they're only charging fifty cents each for those."

Mia and Alexis made me feel better. I think Emma felt better too.

Then we heard loud music coming from the other side of the parking lot. It was dance music, just like I'd heard in the clothing store the night before. We all turned our heads at the same time.

The PGC had set up their booth!

"Let's get a closer look," Mia suggested.

We walked across the parking lot. I hated to admit it, but the PGC booth looked really cool. The table was covered with a black cloth with silver stars dangling from it. There were glittery makeup cases all over the table. They had a banner (the printed kind you order from the store) tied to the canopy up above. It read PGC'S MAKEOVER MAGIC.

"What exactly are they doing?" I wondered out loud.

We walked even closer. Sydney and Bella were busy spreading out makeup and brushes and stuff on the table. Bella had a small sign on the table in front of her that said, GOTH MAKEOVERS ARE MY SPECIALITY. She was wearing a black dress with a poufy skirt. Her reddish-brown hair was pulled back in a sleek ponytail, and her face looked kind of pale. Smudgy dark makeup ringed her eyes.

Next to her, Sydney wore her long blond hair straight and sleek. She was wearing a long white T-shirt over a gray tank with black leggings and boots. It reminded me of an outfit that Mia might wear.

Callie was sitting at a tiny round table set up next to them with a cash box behind her. I noticed that she was dressed exactly the same as Sydney.

So was Maggie. She looked as perfect as Sydney and Callie, except that a long lock of frizzy brown hair was hanging over her eyes. She darted through the crowd, handing out "Makeover Magic" flyers.

"Flyers! Why didn't we think of that?" Alexis said with a frown.

"We don't need flyers to sell cupcakes," Mia said. "Cupcakes sell themselves."

The PGC booth worried me. I mean, it looked really good, a lot better than our table with its cardboard sign. Maybe Sydney had been right all along—they were going to win the contest with their secret weapon.

"Speaking of selling cupcakes, we should get back to the booth," Alexis said.

That's when Maggie bumped into us.

"Oh, hi," she said, shoving a flyer into my hand. "When things get slow at your cupcake stand, stop by for a makeover."

"We'll try, but I don't think things are going to get slow," I said.

We walked away, determined more than ever to sell every last one of our cupcakes.

"The PGC might have music and flyers and glitter, but we have delicious cupcakes!" I cheered. "Let's go win this contest!"

We ran back to our cupcake booth just as the fund-raiser officially opened. A bunch of people came in all at once. We were right by the front entrance, which was a good thing. Almost everybody stopped to check us out. They said nice things like "Wow, it's the school colors!" and "What nice cupcakes!"

But for the first few minutes, nobody bought one.

Then Mrs. Moore, my math teacher, came to the table.

I almost didn't recognize her. When she's teaching us, she wears skirts and blouses and dark colors. Her hair is mostly gray and she always has it pulled back.

But today she was wearing a sweatshirt with a teddy bear on it and jeans. Her hair was loose and went down to the top of her shoulders. I thought it looked nice that way.

"Hello, Miss Brown," she said. She looked at the table. "It must have been a lot of work to make all of these cupcakes."

"There are more in boxes," I told her. "We made two hundred. Well, two hundred and four, actually. That's seventeen dozen."

I was hoping my math would impress her, and maybe it did.

"I'll take one, please," she said, and handed me two dollars in exchange for a cupcake. She took a bite right in front of me.

"Vanilla!" she said. "My favorite."

Then she walked away.

I couldn't believe it. "It's our first sale!" I cried. Everyone let out a cheer. I turned over the money to Alexis, who was in charge of the cash box.

Mrs. Moore must have brought us good luck, because we started selling cupcakes like crazy after that. Some people asked for blue, some people asked for yellow, but most people didn't care which ones they got.

We were so busy selling cupcakes that I forgot about the PGC booth—until a friend of Mia's came to our table. I recognized her as one of the girls Mia talks to in the hallway.

"Hi, Sophie," Mia said. Then she gave a little gasp.

I turned away from the cupcakes to see what had startled Mia. Then I noticed—Sophie's face looked really strange. Her skin had so much white makeup on it that she looked like a clown. The dark makeup around her eyes was smudged everywhere.

"I know," Sophie said, noticing Mia's face. "It's terrible, isn't it? And it cost me five dollars!"

That's when I realized—Sophie was a victim of the Makeover Magic booth!

"It's not so bad," Mia said.

"I was hoping to look pale and mysterious, but this is too much." Sophie sighed. "You should see what's going on over there. It's more like Makeover *Tragic* than Makeover Magic."

Mia and I looked at each other. Then I turned to Emma.

"Can you and Alexis handle things for a minute?" I asked.

Emma nodded. "No problem."

We quickly made our way to the PGC booth. A big crowd had gathered around.

"Maybe Sophie just got unlucky," I said. "It looks like they're doing great."

We inched our way closer so we could get a better view. I realized that most of the crowd wasn't in line to get a makeover. Instead they were watching the action at the booth.

Sydney swiped a brush across the face of a girl sitting across from her.

"There," she said. "You're ready for the runway!"

The girl turned around, and a few people giggled. I tried not to laugh myself. Sydney had put so much fake tanner on the girl that her face looked like a tangerine. Glittery blue eye shadow covered her eyelids.

"I don't know much about fashion, but that doesn't look right to me," I said to Mia.

"That shouldn't look right to *anybody*," Mia whispered back.

"Okay!" Sydney called out. "Who's next?"

Nobody stirred. Then the girl with the orange face nudged her friend. "You promised you would get one if I got one."

The friend looked terrified, but she knew she had to go through with it. She slowly walked up to Callie and handed her five dollars.

"Thanks," Callie said with a smile. But I know Callie really well, and behind that smile I knew she wasn't really happy. I felt just a little bad for her.

The crowd thinned out, and Callie noticed me and Mia standing there.

"Hey, Katie," she called out. "Do you want a makeover?"

"Um, you know I don't wear makeup," I said. "Sorry. You should come check out our cupcake table. I bet your dad would like one. They're vanilla."

A woman I didn't know tapped me on the shoulder. She wore sunglasses and her brown hair was swept back in a tan scarf with designs on it.

"Did you make the cupcakes with the school colors?" she asked.

"Yes—I mean, we did," I said. "We have a club. The Cupcake Club."

"They were beautiful *and* delicious," she said. "Made from scratch, I could tell. I would love to have you make some for the PTA luncheon this spring. We'd pay you, of course."

Mia and I exchanged glances. Someone wanted to pay us to make cupcakes. Just like professionals. How awesome was that?

Maggie flew up to the woman. "Mom! The Cupcake Club is a *rival* booth! You're consorting with the enemy."

"Calm down, Maggie," her mom said. "It's all for the school. I was just coming to get my makeover."

Maggie glared at us, but I didn't care. I was feeling pretty good.

Then Callie stood up. "Maggie, can you work the cash box for a minute? I'm going to get a cupcake."

Sydney dropped the makeup brush she was holding. "Callie, you absolutely *cannot* buy a cupcake. Do you want to win this contest or not?"

"It's just a cupcake," Callie said quietly.

Callie walked over. We smiled at each other.

Maybe Callie was right. Maybe it was just a cupcake.

But to me, it felt like so much more.

CHAPTER 18

The Icing on the Cupcake

The fund-raiser ended at three o'clock, and by then we had sold almost every single cupcake. Then Mia's stepdad, Eddie, came to pick her up.

"Hey, girls," he said, smiling big. "How did the cupcake sales go?"

"Great," Mia told him.

Alexis counted the remaining cupcakes. "We sold one hundred and eighty-three," she reported.

"So that means you have seventeen left?" he asked.

Alexis nodded.

"Tell you what," Eddie said. He took his wallet from his pocket. "I've got a big meeting on Monday. I bet everyone at work would like some cupcakes. I'll take everything you have left."

"Wow, thanks!" I said.

"That will be thirty-four dollars, please," Alexis said matter-of-factly.

Mia smiled. "Thanks, Eddie," she said, and she looked really happy. "You didn't have to do that."

"I did," said Eddie. "I'm making them all work late, but they don't know it yet!" He laughed. I still couldn't tell how Mia felt about Eddie, but he seemed nice enough to me. I wondered what it would be like if Mom got married again. That would be weird. Too weird to think about.

Thanks to Eddie, we sold every single one of our cupcakes. We turned over our four hundred dollars to Principal LaCosta. Then we headed home to get ready for the dance that night.

I put on my new purple dress and Mia's black boots. I checked out my reflection in the mirror. I still didn't feel like I could be in a magazine or anything. But I thought I looked pretty good.

Mom got teary-eyed when I came downstairs.

"My baby's first dance," she said, gripping me in a hug. "Oh, you look so glamorous!"

"Mo-om," I said in a complaining voice. (But to be honest, I kind of liked it.)

We picked up Mia, who of course looked great, and then Mom dropped us off. The gym was decorated just like you see in the movies or on TV. There were more blue and yellow balloons and streamers, and a DJ was set up over by the basketball hoop. I was happy to see that Alexis and Emma were there already, over by the food table.

"Wow, you look nice," Emma said.

"So do you guys," I replied. "So, what's to eat?"

"There's punch, some vegetable platters, and cupcakes," Alexis reported.

Emma groaned. "I don't think I can look at another cupcake today."

"I can *always* look at a cupcake," I said, examining the trays. They looked normal—chocolate with chocolate icing, and I could tell the icing came from a can.

"Speaking of cupcakes," Alexis said. "I talked to my parents at dinner about our PTA cupcake order. You know, they're accountants, so they can help us figure out what to charge so we make a profit. They said they could even set us up as a business if we want."

"Our own business?" I asked. I hadn't thought about our little Cupcake Club as anything more than . . . well, making and eating cupcakes. But making money, too? That couldn't be bad. "I like it!"

"I could design the logo!" said Mia.

"I bet I could make more than I do babysitting my brother!" said Emma excitedly. "I'm in!"

"Then," proclaimed Alexis, "we are officially the Cupcake Club. Open for business!"

"Yay!" We all laughed and went in for a group hug. It felt good. For the first time in a while I wasn't really worrying about anything. Not Callie. Not middle school. Not even math.

Then some girls I didn't know came up to us.

"Those cupcakes you made were sooo good," one of the girls said.

"Yeah," said her friend. "How did you make them?"

"It's easy," I said. "You just follow the recipe."

Then a funky beat blared through the gym. "Hey, I love this song!" Mia said. Before I could say no, she grabbed my arm and dragged me onto the dance floor. Alexis and Emma followed us. We danced to the whole song, and then the next one.

George Martinez was dancing by himself. He pointed at me.

"Hey, Silly Arms!"

I started waving my arms around like the Silly Arms sprinkler. George cracked up. Then Mia started doing it too.

"Hey, that's pretty fun!" she said.

Then the gym got quiet. Principal LaCosta walked up to the DJ and took the microphone from him.

"Students, welcome to Park Street's first dance of the year!" she cried, and a bunch of people cheered and whistled. "Now it's time to announce the winners of our first contest. The winning table today raised four hundred dollars for our school."

Alexis gasped. It still wasn't sinking in with me, though. Not until Principal LaCosta called our name.

"Let's hear it for the Cupcake Club!"

Emma let out a loud squeal. Then I realized I was squealing too. We won! We actually won! It was like the sweet icing on top of a delicious cupcake.

The four of us ran up to the DJ booth and Principal LaCosta handed us our prize. "Congratulations, girls! You've each won a Park Street Middle School sweatshirt!"

Everyone clapped. I still couldn't believe it. Then the DJ started to blast the song, "Celebrate!"

Mia draped the sweatshirt over her shoulders. "Victory dance!" she yelled.

Just then Callie ran up to me and gave me a big hug.

"Katie, that's so awesome!" she said.

Then we both stopped, stared at each other, and

started to laugh. We were both wearing the same dress! I had forgotten that purple was Callie's favorite color.

"You look great!" she said.

"You do too!" I laughed. I wondered if Sydney told Callie she thought the dress was ugly.

Mia, Alexis, and Emma were running out to the dance floor. I didn't know I was doing it, but I must have been following them with my eyes. A kind of sad smile crossed Callie's face.

"Go dance with your friends," she said.

Callie was the one who said we should make new friends in middle school. When she first said that, I was hurt. But she was right. It felt good to have new friends, but it felt good to have old friends, too.

"Come dance with us," I said.

Callie shook her head. "No, you go. I'll call you tomorrow, okay?"

"Okay," I told her, moving toward the club. Then I looked back. I saw her walking toward Sydney, Maggie, and Bella. Sydney did not look happy.

"Hey, Callie!" I called. She turned around. "I'm glad we're friends!" I yelled. I said it loud, so she could hear it over the music. But I also said it so Sydney could hear me.

"Me too!" Callie called back, and then walked toward the PGC.

I ran off to dance with the Cupcake Club. As I waved my silly arms in the air, I realized something.

The first day of middle school had been awful. Callie had let me down. I got into trouble. Things did not go the way I planned at all.

But the weird thing was that middle school was not a total disaster. Everything had worked out, somehow.

Maybe it was time for a new recipe.

Mix together:
One purple dress.
One corny mom.
Two hundred and four cupcakes.
Three new friends.
One old friend.
Stir gently until they're all blended together.
Then dance.

If you're not an expert baker like Katie, that's okay—here is a quick and easy-to-follow recipe that's just as sweet! (Ask an adult for assistance before you start baking since you might need help with the oven or mixer.)

Pineapple "Upside-Down" Cupcakes

• Makes 18 •

BATTER:
1 box of yellow cake mix
1 cup sour cream
½ cup of pineapple juice (use juice from canned pineapples; see topping)
⅓ cup vegetable oil
4 large eggs, room temperature
1 teaspoon pure vanilla extract

TOPPING:
8 tablespoons unsalted butter, melted
¾ cup firmly packed light brown sugar
1 can (20 ounces) crushed pineapple, drained (set aside ½ cup of the pineapple juice for batter)
maraschino cherries (optional)

Center baking rack in oven and preheat to 350°F. Grease cupcake tins well with butter or cooking spray.

CUPCAKES: In a large mixing bowl combine all of the batter ingredients. With an electric mixer on medium speed, mix the ingredients together until there are no lumps in the batter. Spoon the batter into the cupcake tins so that each tin is about halfway full.

TOPPING: Mix the melted butter and brown sugar together with a spoon. Sprinkle about a teaspoon of the mixture on top of the cupcake batter in the tins. Now add a layer of about a tablespoon of pineapple. If you'd like, put one cherry on top, pressing it into the pineapple layer so it's level.

Bake the cupcakes about 18 to 20 minutes or until a toothpick inserted into the center of a cupcake comes out clean. Remove from oven and place on a wire rack to cool for about 5 minutes. Carefully run a dinner knife around the edges of the cupcakes and invert the cupcake pan onto the wire rack. Let the cupcakes cool for about 20 minutes.

yummy! :

Want another sweet cupcake?

Here's a sneak peek
of the second book in the

CUPCAKE DIARIES

series:

Mia
in the mix

An *Interesting* Remark

My name is Mia Vélaz-Cruz, and I hate Mondays.

I know, everybody says that, right? But I think I have some very compelling reasons for hating Mondays.

For example, every other weekend I go to Manhattan to see my dad. My parents are divorced, and my mom and I moved out to a town in the suburbs, an hour outside the city. I really like living with my mom, but I miss my dad a lot. I miss Manhattan, too, and all of my friends there. On the weekends I visit my dad, he drives me back to my mom's house late on Sunday nights. So it's weird when I wake up on Monday and I realize I'm not in New York anymore. Every two weeks I wake up all confused, which is not a good way to start a Monday.

Another reason I don't like Mondays is that it's the first day of the school week. That means five days of school until I get a day off. Five days of Mrs. Moore's hard math quizzes. And I have to wait all the way till the end of the week for Cupcake Friday. That's the day that either I or one of my friends brings in cupcakes to eat at lunch. That's how we formed the Cupcake Club. But I'll tell you more about that in a minute.

Lately I've been looking over a bunch of journal entries, and I've realized that when annoying things happen, they usually happen on a Monday. Back in May, my mom told me on a Monday night that we were moving out of New York. When I ruined my new suede boots because of a sudden rainstorm, it was on a Monday. And the last time I lost my cell phone, it was Monday. And when did I find it? Friday, of course. Because Friday is an awesome day.

Then there was that bad Monday I had a few weeks ago. It should have been a good Monday. A *great* Monday, even, because that was my first day back at school after the Cupcake Club won the contest.

Remember when I mentioned Cupcake Club? I'm in the club with my friends Katie, Alexis, and Emma. It started because we all eat lunch together, and on the first day of school Katie brought in this amazing peanut-butter-and-jelly cupcake that her mom made. Katie is a fabulous cupcake baker too, and she and her mom taught us all how to make them, so we decided to form our own club and make them together. Fun, right?

A little while after we formed the club, Principal LaCosta announced there was going to be a contest the day of the first school dance. There would be a big fund-raising fair in the school parking lot, and the group that raised the most funds would win a prize at the dance.

We hadn't really planned on participating in the fund-raiser, but then this other group in our class, the Popular Girls Club, kept telling everyone they were going to win. The leader of the group, Sydney, bragged that they had some "top-secret" idea that was going to blow everyone away. It's not like we're rivals or anything, but once we heard that, we decided to enter the contest too. Our idea was to sell cupcakes decorated with the school colors (that part was my idea).

The PGC's big secret ended up being a makeover booth, which would have been a cool idea except they weren't very good at doing makeovers. In fact, they were terrible at it. But we were very good at baking cupcakes. We sold two hundred cupcakes and won the contest. At the dance that night, Principal LaCosta gave us our prizes: four Park Street Middle School sweatshirts.

I know it's not a huge deal or anything, but it felt really good to win. Back at my old school, things were really competitive. Just about every kid took singing lessons or art lessons or violin lessons or French lessons. Everyone was good at something. It was hard to stand out there, and I never won a prize before. I was really happy that we won. It made me think maybe it wasn't bad that we moved out here.

Just before my mom picked me up the night of our big win, Alexis had an idea.

"We should all wear our sweatshirts to school on Monday," she said.

"Isn't that kind of like bragging?" Emma asked.

"We should do it," Katie said. "All the football guys wear their jerseys when they win a game. We won. We should be proud."

"Yes, definitely," I agreed. I mean, Katie was right. We should be proud. Making two hundred cupcakes is a lot of work!

Except for one problem. I don't do sweatshirts. I'm sorry, but the last time I wore one I was five, and it made me look like a steamed dumpling. They are all lumpy and the sleeves are always too long.

Even though I wanted to show how proud I was of winning, I also knew there was no way I could wear that sweatshirt on Monday. I really care about what I wear, probably because my mom used to work for a big fashion magazine. So fashion is in my blood. But I also think clothes are a fun way to express yourself. You can seriously tell a lot about a person by what they choose to wear, like their mood for instance. And so to *me* a sweatshirt just says "I'm in the mood to sweat!"

I told Mom about my sweatshirt issue on the drive home.

"Mia, I'm surprised by you," she said. "You're great at transforming your old clothes into new and amazing creations. Think of your old school uniform. You made that look great and like you every day. If you *had* to wear a sweatshirt, I'd bet you could come up with something really cool and great."

Mom was right, to be honest, and I was a little surprised I hadn't thought of it first. Our old school uniform was terrible: ugly plaid skirts with plain white, itchy tops. But you could wear a sweater or a jacket and any shoes, so you could get pretty creative with it and not look gross on a daily basis. That's one of the good things about my new school—you can wear whatever you want. Inspired, I sat at my sewing table the next day and cut up the sweatshirt. I turned it into a cool hobo bag, the kind with a big pouch and a long strap. I added a few cool studs to the strap and around the school logo to funk it up a little. I was really proud of how it looked.

On Monday morning I picked out an outfit to go with the bag: a denim skirt, a blue knit shirt with a brown leather belt around the waist, and a dark-gray-and-white-striped-blazer. I rolled up the sleeves of the blazer, then put the bag over my shoulder and checked out my reflection in the long mirror attached to my closet.

Too much blue, I decided. I changed the blue shirt to a white one, then changed the belt to a braided silver belt and checked again.

Better, I thought. I pulled my long black hair back into a ponytail. *Maybe a headband . . . or maybe braid it to the side . . .*

"Mia! You'll be late for your bus!" Mom called from downstairs.

I sighed. I'm almost always late for the bus, no matter how early I wake up. I decided to leave my hair down and hurried downstairs.

Taking a bus to school is something I still need

to get used to. When I went to my school in New York, I took the subway. A lot of people don't like the subway because of how crowded it is, but I love it. I like to study the people and see what they're wearing. Everyone has their own distinct style and things that they're into. And there are all kinds of people on a subway—old people, moms with little kids, kids going to school like me, people from the suburbs going to work. Also, on the subway, nobody whispers about you behind your back like they do on the bus. Nobody makes loud burping noises either, like Wes Kinney does every single day in the back of the school bus, which is extremely disgusting.

The best thing about the bus, though, is that my friend Katie takes it with me. That's how we met, on the first day of school. Her best friend was supposed to ride with her, but she walked to school instead, so I asked Katie to sit with me. I felt bad for Katie, but it was lucky for me. Katie is really cool.

When Katie got on the bus that morning she was wearing her Park Street sweatshirt with lightly ripped jeans and her favorite blue canvas sneakers. Her wavy brown hair was down. She has natural highlights, as if she hung out every day at the beach.

If I didn't know Katie, I would have guessed she was from California.

"Hey!" Katie said, sliding into the seat next to me. She pointed to her sweatshirt. "I still can't believe we won!"

"Me either," I said. "But we did make some really fabulous cupcakes."

"Totally," Katie agreed. Then she frowned. "Did you forget to wear your shirt?"

"I'm wearing it," I told her. I showed her the bag. "What do you think?"

"No way!" Katie grabbed it to get a closer look. "Did your mom do this?"

"I did," I replied.

"That is awesome," Katie said. "I didn't know you could sew. That's got to be harder than making cupcakes."

I shrugged. "I don't know. It just takes practice."

Braaap! Wes Kinney made a big fake burp just then. His friends all started laughing.

"That is so gross," Katie said, shaking her head.

"Seriously!" I agreed.

This Monday was starting out okay (except for the part when I didn't get to wear my headband). But it got annoying pretty fast in homeroom.

None of my Cupcake Club friends are in my

homeroom, but I do know some kids. There's George Martinez, who's kind of cute and really funny. He's in my science and social studies classes too. There's Sophie, who I like a lot. But she sits next to her best friend, Lucy, and in homeroom they're always in a huddle, whispering to each other.

Then there is Sydney Whitman and Callie Wilson. Sydney is the one who started the Popular Girls Club. Callie is in the club too, and she's also the girl who used to be Katie's best friend. I can see why, because she's nice, like Katie.

Katie, Alexis, and Emma all think Sydney is horrible. They say she's always making mean comments to them. She's never said anything really mean to me. And to be honest, I like the way she dresses. She has a really good sense of fashion, which is something we have in common. Like today, she was wearing a scoop-neck T-shirt with a floral chiffon skirt, black leggings, and an awesome wraparound belt that had a large pewter flower as the buckle. So sometimes I think, you know, that maybe we could be friends. Don't get me wrong—the girls in the Cupcake Club are my BFFs, and I love them. But none of them are into fashion the way I am.

Sydney and Callie sit right across from me. Callie gave me a smile when I sat down.

"Those were great cupcakes you guys made on Saturday," Callie told me.

"Thanks," I said.

I thought I saw Sydney give Callie a glare. But when she turned to me, she was smiling too.

"That was a really *interesting* dress you wore to the dance, Mia," Sydney said.

Hmm. I wasn't sure what "interesting" meant. I had worn a minidress with black, purple, and turquoise panels, a black sequined jacket, and black patent leather peep toe flats. "Perfectly chic," my mom had said.

"Thanks."

"Very . . . red carpet maybe?" Sydney went on. "Although, I was reading this really *interesting* article in *Fashionista* magazine all about choosing the right outfit for the right event. You know, like how being *overdressed* can be just as bad as being underdressed."

I knew exactly what Sydney was doing. She was insulting me, but in a "nice" way. Sort of. I know my outfit might have been a little too sophisticated for a middle school dance, but so what? I liked it.

"There's no such thing as being overdressed," I replied calmly. "That's what my mom taught me. She used to be an editor at *Flair* magazine." Then

I opened up my notebook and began to sketch. I don't normally brag about my mother's job like that, but I didn't know what to say to Sydney.

"Wow!" said Callie. "*Flair*? That's so cool! Isn't that cool?" She turned to Sydney, who looked uninterested. "We read that all the time at Sydney's house. Her mom gets it."

Sydney opened her math book and pretended to start reading.

"You looked really great!" said Callie, like she was trying to make up for Sydney. I honestly didn't really care if they liked it or not. I thought I looked good and that outfit made me feel great.

I wasn't mad at Sydney—just annoyed. Which is not a fabulous way to start the day.

But what can you expect from a Monday?

Still Hungry?
There's always room for another Cupcake!

Katie and the Cupcake Cure **1**

Mia in the Mix **2**

Emma on Thin Icing **3**

Alexis and the Perfect Recipe **4**

Katie, Batter Up! **5**

Mia's Baker's Dozen **6**

Emma All Stirred Up! **7**

Alexis Cool as a Cupcake **8**

Katie and the Cupcake War **9**

Mia's Boiling Point **10**

Emma, Smile and Say "Cupcake!" **11**

Alexis Gets Frosted **12**

Katie's New Recipe **13**

Mia a Matter of Taste **14**